Finders Keepers

Dorothy A. Winsor

Copyright © 2016 Dorothy A. Winsor

All rights reserved.

ISBN: **1537198831**
ISBN-13: **978-1537198835**

DEDICATION

For Nilmandra

1. THE GIFT

A game! A game! Come play.—Cild, the child god

"Cut it out, Cade." Eyes glued to his book, Roth caught the warrior game piece I'd slid across the table and flicked it back to me.

"Don't you want to play war?" I pinged a second warrior off the lantern glowing next to Roth's book.

My brother turned a page of *Property Law in Midland* and kept reading. He'd had his nose in that book since he brought it home from the law office where he was apprenticed.

"Are you shining up to that lawyer?" I asked. "If Duval let you borrow that book, he must like you."

Roth looked up. "Unlike your boss?" He grinned and leaned back, stretching his feet out so they were under my stool. My brother was long-legged and broad-shouldered. I'd be that way too once I had my growth spurt, though that was taking its time showing up. "What have you been up to, Cade?" Roth asked.

I glanced toward Mum. She'd worked at the neighborhood laundry all day, and despite how late it was, now she sewed at the mending she took in. The fire in the brazier turned her heart-shaped face pink on one side.

"I didn't do anything," I said quickly. "Master Joff was just crabby."

"But what was Master Joff crabby about?" Roth lifted the hair out of his eyes.

"Nothing." I kicked his ankle. I liked working with the horses at Master Joff's stable, and when I got old enough, he was going to help me enlist as a soldier. He said I was scrappy enough to be a good one, but today, after I ran out to look at a wagon that tipped over at Five Corners, he said I needed a sergeant to kick my backside. Anyone would call that crabby.

"Leave him alone, Roth," Mum said, "and remind me to cut your hair tomorrow." She bit off a thread and folded the shirt she'd been working on. Then she reached into her basket for a ragged sock the size of a bucket. "What do you two want for New Year? There'll be parties in all the big houses, and if I finish this mending on time, we can afford to celebrate a little too. Reaching the year 4000 is worth doing something special."

New Year was my favorite holiday, and it was only three weeks away on the first day of spring, but I felt bad that Mum was doing extra work. "We could get a dog," I said. "It wouldn't even cost anything. The dog at the stable has puppies."

Roth rolled his eyes.

"You know the landlord won't allow it," Mum said.

"We could hide it when he comes," I said.

"No," Mum said. "And we're out of water."

"I could train it to hide under my bed." I fetched the water bucket from its corner and started for the door.

"Wear your cloak," Mum said.

"Oh, Mum," I groaned, then grabbed my cloak from its hook.

"Put it on," Mum called as I shut the door.

It was nearly dark, and the air was cold enough to freeze donkey dung before it plopped onto the road. I scuttled along for half a block before I set the bucket down and wrapped my cloak around my shoulders. My breath made clouds that I trotted through on my way to the pump in Twisted Knee Lane. I hoped it was working. For the last few days, water had only trickled out, and I didn't want to have to go all the way to Weasel Alley.

When I got there, I could see someone had dug out the road, exposing a leather-patched pipe surrounded by a pool of water. I set the bucket under the spout and worked the handle. Water gushed out. Good.

I was reaching for the full bucket when something gleamed in the puddle around the pipe. As I crouched to look, a tingle slid over my skin. Was that glitter more than just lamplight reflected from the house across the way? I thrust my hand through a skin of ice into water so cold that my fingers felt like I'd hammered them. Something smooth lay in the mud, something that made my hand feel better the instant I touched it. I fished out a flat, triangular stone with a hole in one corner.

The thing should have been icy from the water, but it felt warm. I stood up, turning it over and over. I couldn't see its color in the dark, but at the edge of my hearing, a woman was singing. When I bent closer, the singing got louder. Was it coming from the stone?

"Cade! Cade!" From our street, Roth's shouts jolted me back to awareness.

I shoved the stone into my pocket, then grabbed the heavy bucket and hurried toward the corner, the bucket bumping my leg and sloshing water.

Roth met me at the corner. "Where have you been? Mum's worried." He took the bucket and started for home. Annoyingly, I had to trot to keep up.

"I haven't been gone that long."

"You have," he said.

I looked up and saw stars. It was full dark. When did that happen?

"What were you doing anyway?" Roth asked.

Inside my pocket, I slid my little finger into the hole in the stone. A happy idea jumped into my head. Mum could thread the stone onto a bootlace and wear it around her neck. "You'll see," I said.

"See what?" He shoved our door open.

Face pinched with worry, Mum looked up from her mending.

"He's all right," Roth said. "He was just dawdling." He flicked a finger at my ear.

I dodged out of his reach. "Put out your hand," I told Mum.

She raised an eyebrow but did as I asked. Keeping the stone hidden in my hand, I pulled it out of my pocket. I held it over her palm, watching her face to see how pleased she'd be. For a moment, it was like the stone was stuck to my hand. In that bit of time, Mum's eyes widened, and she drew in a sharp breath just as I managed at last to drop the stone. A wave of dizziness washed through my head. The stone teetered on her fingers, then slid into her grip. In the flickering lantern light, the stone glowed red and transparent as glass.

Mum rose so fast that she dropped the sock.

"What's the matter?" Roth charged up next to me and took Mum's arm. "What did you give her, Cade?"

Mum showed him.

He took a step backward. "A heart stone," he whispered.

Of course! I should have known from the way it eased my aching fingers. But I'd seen a heart stone only one other time, and it had been stuck in a shrine where it couldn't heal people any more because someone had given it back to the gods. Heart stones sweetened the life in a land, a body, or a house. Fancy healers used them, and rich folks kept them in their houses for good fortune.

"Where did you get this?" Mum asked.

"I found it," I said. "I saw something where they'd dug around that pump, and when I looked, there it was."

The only sound was an ember clunking to the bottom of the brazier.

"Tricky gods." Roth sounded like he was strangling. "You're a Finder."

"I am not!" My heart thumped harder. Everyone knew Finders sniffed out heart stones and then went stone mad when they were around them too long. The miners took charge of Finders, letting them hunt for heart stones so they wouldn't go completely off their heads, and keeping them away from the rest of us. I was not a Finder.

"I'm so sorry, Cade." Mum's voice broke. "Roth is all right, and when you turned twelve with no trouble, I thought you were too."

"Let me get rid of that, Mum." Roth reached for the stone, but Mum cradled it against her breast and backed away.

"Why do we have to get rid of it?" I asked. "It doesn't belong to anyone. It was just lying there under the pump. Why can't we keep it?" I tried to touch the bit of stone peeking through Mum's fingers, but she wouldn't let me.

"All those stones come from the Half-Wit Hills." Still watching Mum, Roth waved toward the law book he'd just been reading. "Unless you buy them, they belong to the miners, whether they're dug out or wash down the rivers. But that's not the only problem with it being here. Mum, please! Let me take it."

Mum took a noisy gulp of air. "No. I'll do it. You stay with Cade." She slid past Roth and fumbled with her cloak.

"What are you going to do?" Roth lowered the hand he'd been holding out.

"Leave it in the shrine in Long Street," Mum said. "Unless—Cade, can you put it in the shrine?"

"Why should we do that? We should keep it. It can heal us and stuff." Roth groaned, and I glared at him. "I don't care what that book says. I didn't steal it."

"Please," Mum said. "If you give it back to the gods, you give back the gift of Finding too."

"Finding's not a gift," I said, "and I'm not a Finder. I just think we should keep the stone. Think how good it would have been if we'd had it when Dad got sick." And if the stone was in our house, I could touch it and listen to it sing whenever I wanted. It seemed best not to say that though. Mum looked set on not letting me near it.

She took a deep breath and buttoned her cloak. "Being around heart stones has made me stone sick off and on for a long time." Mum's voice trembled. "The need will go once I've left the stone."

"Are you sure you can do it?" Roth said.

"It's been years since I touched a stone," Mum said. "I've grown strong enough to resist a stone's call. I know I have." At the door, Mum looked over her shoulder at Roth. "If things go wrong, if I'm not back by morning, promise me you'll take Cade and leave the city."

"What are you saying?" I cried. "How could we leave you?"

Roth opened and closed his mouth. "I..."

"Promise me, Roth," Mum said.

Roth jerked a nod.

Mum hurried out, slamming the door.

I spun to face Roth. "What's she talking about? Roth, what's happening?"

He drew his hand down his face, stretching his cheeks. "She's a Finder, idiot, which is why you are."

"She's not! And I'm not either."

He shook his head. "Didn't you see how she held on to that heart stone?"

I pictured Mum's hands, wrapped around the triangular stone. She wouldn't let anyone else touch it, much less have it. Could Roth be right? I staggered back and fell onto my stool. "She's stone mad? But...but Mum would never hurt anyone."

"Stone madness isn't like what people say." Roth paced the room. He was still wearing his cloak, and it swirled out behind him. "And she's not really mad, but she shouldn't be near a heart stone. Neither should you, if only because we don't want anyone to see what you are. Not unless you want to wind up in a heart stone mine." He paced some more, while I stared at the sock on the floor and wrestled to put Mum and Finders in the same place in my head.

And me. If Roth was right, I belonged there too. I rose to pick up the sock, stuck the needle into it, and set it carefully on Mum's bench.

"Once she puts it in the shrine, she won't be mad anymore," I said. "Not that she's really mad anyway."

"If she puts it in the shrine. And if the Watch doesn't nab her." Roth stopped with his thumb on the door latch. "You wait here. I want to be sure she's all right."

"I'm not staying here while Mum's in trouble." I started after him, but he shoved me back onto the stool.

"Shut up, and do what I say," Roth said. "Don't you get it? You can't be near that stone." He was out of the house before I'd drawn breath enough to tell him where to put his do-what-I-say stuff.

I bounced to my feet and went after him.

2. AT THE SHRINE

Be a shield to your home, a sword to its enemies.—Sceld, the hero god

    I was quick, but by the time I got outside, Roth was nowhere in sight. With my feet skittering on frozen ruts, I raced around the corner, down Bent Creek Lane, and around another corner into Long Street. Halfway down the block, where the shrine was, a shadow moved in the dark. Mum? No. I knew that bow-legged, skinny figure. Beam, the Watchman who patrolled our neighborhood. I stopped so suddenly that I skidded on a patch of ice. I tried to back around the corner.

"Halt!" Beam called.

Heart thundering in my chest, I waited while he hustled toward me.

Three yards away, he slowed and lowered his club. Starlight flashed off his metal-studded leather vest. "Cade? You're out late. Does your mum know where you are?"

"She sent me to borrow lamp oil from Mistress Berta." I pointed past him down Long Street, then saw how my hand was shaking and tucked it in my pocket.

"You don't have a jar," Beam said.

"Mum said Mistress Berta will give me one," I said.

"Shall I check that with your mum?" Beam asked.

"Sure."

Beam bent closer and studied my face. I opened my eyes wide and thought innocent thoughts.

"All right." Bean straightened. "On your way." He jerked his thumb over his shoulder, and I walked past him.

Don't look back. Only someone guilty would look back. My head tried to turn anyway.

Beam's footsteps crunched into the distance. I passed the shrine without looking in, went another few yards, and risked glancing over my shoulder. Beam was gone.

I ran back toward the shrine. Just as I reached it, a big, black shape lunged out of the gap between the shrine and a house. I opened my mouth to shout for Beam, but the big shape clapped a hand around my jaw.

"Don't," Roth said.

I steadied my shaking legs and shoved his hand away. "Where's Mum?"

"I don't know." Roth stepped into the shelter of the shrine, ducking under the carved symbols of the eight gods and touching the symbol of Lerned the Wise, the way he always did. I touched Sceld the Hero. We needed him now. Judging by how smooth he was worn, lots of folks did.

Inside the half shell of rock, I squinted through the dark to make out the offerings on the shelf—a small clay bowl, a yarn doll, a pebble that was probably pretty in daylight. No triangular heart stone, and if she'd left it, it would still be here. Once those stones went into a shrine, they couldn't be pried out.

"She hasn't been here yet?" I said. "How can that be?"

"Maybe she's waiting back behind the shops for Beam to pass," Roth said, "or she's somewhere working up her courage. Plum Tree Lane, maybe. She likes the way there are always birds in the gardens along there. But Beam'll be back before long. His round ends at the fish mongers."

"You look behind the shops," I said. "I'll check the Lane."

He grabbed the back of my cloak. "You stay with me."

"But—"

He yanked, and the cloak cut hard into my throat. "You and Mum together with that stone? I don't think so. Come on."

He bundled me across Long Street and up three blocks to Plum Tree Lane. Then he pointed for me to search the left side while he searched the right. I hurried along, calling Mum softly and looking in every gap or space where someone could huddle. I couldn't believe we had to do this. Would Mum actually hide from us?

Off to the right, a dog barked a warning. Someone must be passing its yard. Beam maybe? At this time of night, that was most likely.

"She's not here," Roth called softly, swerving left around a corner. "We'll check the shops." I ran to catch up. We hurried down a street snaking back toward the shrine and the shops behind it. Something warm brushed across my chest. I wanted it.

I put a hand on Roth's arm. "I feel the stone."

"Which way?" Roth said sharply.

I turned in a complete circle. "I'm not sure." I took another step toward the shrine and halted. A shadow moved in the alley across Long

Street. It froze, then moved again, creeping nearer the shrine.

I staggered toward it, but Roth gripped my cloak again. "Wait. Be sure it's her."

"I'm sure," I said.

The shadow came out of the alley and turned into Mum. I breathed easily for what felt like the first time since I left the house. She was all right. She'd only been slow getting here. She stopped, her hands against her chest, hiding what she held. She faced the shrine but made no move toward it. My throat clogged. I knew how she felt. I wanted to keep the stone too. But she was stone mad. She couldn't keep it.

"We have to help her." I pulled against Roth's hold.

"She has to do it freely." Roth flicked me a look. "And you have to stay away."

Mum took one step toward the shrine, and then another. She gulped a breath deep enough that I saw her shoulders rise and fall. Then stretching out a hand that surely held the stone, she moved into the doorway of the shrine. She was an arm's length from the altar, an arm's length from being well.

"Halt," a man's voice called.

Beam.

"What are you doing there?" He charged into sight. "What do you have? Mareth, is that you?"

With a curse, Roth let go of me and started toward Mum. She tried to scramble back away from Beam, but her foot slid on an icy patch and she fell.

I broke into a run. Roth must have heard me because he whirled and grabbed me around the waist.

"Let me go!" I writhed in his arms.

He got a hand free and clapped it over my mouth again, pressing it against my teeth so hard that I tasted blood. "You can't. You can't." He shook me. "You understand? You can't."

I wanted to help Mum. I wanted the stone! Doubt blew through me. Which was it?

Beam bent over Mum. "Let me see what you have."

I pushed Roth's hand from my mouth. "Help her," I whispered. "I'll stay here."

He bolted toward Long Street. "Beam! What's going on? Did she fall?"

Beam was trying to pull Mum's hands open so he could see what she had. Gods help us. Mum was crying. The noise of it tore my heart out. I crept closer, staying in the shadows on the edge of the street. At the limit of my hearing, the stone sang.

"Get out of here, Roth," Beam said grimly.

"What's the matter?" Roth said. "Let me take her home." He reached for Mum, but Beam clubbed him on the shoulder. Roth grunted, but kept trying to get hold of Mum.

"Don't hurt him!" Mum cried. "Here. Have it, Beam." She held out the heart stone.

"You can let her go now," Roth babbled. "She's giving you the stone, so that's all right. She just had it by accident."

Ignoring Roth, Beam tried to pry the stone out of Mum's hands. When she held on, he hit her fingers hard enough that Mum cried out and dropped the stone.

I jumped out of hiding and onto Beam's back.

"Cade, no!" Mum said.

With a roar, Beam grabbed my arm and flung me to the ground. The stars swirled overhead. I tried to blink away the darkness closing in around my vision.

Roth hauled Mum to her feet and pushed her away. "Run!"

She took one step, then slid to her knees on the ice, groping for the stone.

Beam seized her arm, hauled her up, and pointed his club toward Roth and me. "Enough! Both of you, get away, or I can't promise she won't be hurt."

I lurched to my feet and stumbled up next to Roth, who was breathing hard, opening and closing his fists. Fire light gleamed through a barely opened doorway in a house on our right—the neighbors looking to see what the noise was about.

Beam hooked a foot around the heart stone and scooped it toward him, clattering when it bounced over a rut. Still holding Mum, he picked it up and put it in his pocket. "You two go home," he said. "Governor Barth will hear the evidence and sort this out."

Neither Roth nor I moved.

"Go!" Beam prodded his club into Mum's ribs.

"Go," Mum repeated.

"No," Roth said.

"Please," Mum said. "Remember your promise, Roth."

For a moment, Roth held so still, he quivered. Then he groaned, took my arm, and pulled me toward home. I dug in my feet and looked over my shoulder, but Roth was just too strong.

Beam waited until we were at the corner before he turned and led Mum away.

"Mum, we'll come get you!" I cried.

"No," she called back. "Roth, you promised."

Roth dragged me, running faster and faster.

I was crying, and I didn't care if Roth knew. "Where are we going?"

"Home to get our stuff, then out of the city." Roth turned into our street. Through the open window, our lantern and brazier glowed.

"But Mum needs us," I said. "Why do we have to go?"

"Why do you think?" Roth's voice was rough. With a shock, I realized he was crying too. "Finders are worth a fortune to the miners," Roth said. "It runs in families. If Mum's one, we may be too. They'll test us, and they'll take you."

"I don't care."

Roth pushed our door open and shoved me through. "Mum does. And strange as it seems, I do. Get your stuff." He went through into the back room, Mum's room.

I climbed the ladder to our sleeping loft and pulled my carry bag from under my bed. But instead of gathering my belongings, I stood looking over the loft's edge, down at Mum's sewing basket, Roth's book, the game pieces I'd been tossing around. The room smelled of the bean soup we'd had for supper. How could our house still be the same when it felt like my old life was ending?

Roth scrambled up the ladder, carrying the leather pouch holding our marketing money and the smaller one holding Dad's wedding ring. He'd stopped crying. Instead his jaw was set tight enough that a muscle jumped in front of one ear. "Why are you standing there? Move, Cade."

When I still didn't, he touched my shoulder lightly. "Don't worry. We have to go, but not without Mum. After all, we know where to find her."

My gaze met his. His brown eyes were cold and hard as the frozen mud in the street. I started stuffing clothes in my carry bag.

3. THE HEART STONE MINE

Here be monsters.—Sig, the shadow god
At dawn two days later, I crept up the last hill leading to Midland's heart stone mine. I dropped to my belly, pushed a branch aside, and slithered through a tangle of leafless bushes.

Roth slid up beside me, close enough for me to feel the tension in his shoulder. Below us, a stone wall arced out from a steep hillside, fencing in a dark opening that looked nastily like a mouth. A gate blocked it, and the bars looked like teeth. They'd even snagged a bundle of rags. Inside the wall, a guard paced past walking a huge dog with an even nastier mouth and teeth. The guard skirted a row of huts and turned to pace back.

Roth and I watched, blowing on our freezing hands, waiting long enough that snow soaked through my trouser legs. When I shivered, Roth gave me a worried look. "Do you feel the stones?" he asked.

"No." I jerked my arm out from under his concerned touch. "I don't feel anything. Are you sure this is the right place? Maybe they're digging up diamonds or something."

"Mum says the feel of the stones is cut off by a barrier, especially if the stone is small," Roth said. "So the hillside is sheltering you, but promise you'll tell me if you feel anything."

"I'm fine! Just cold. Stop fussing before I get you a frilly cap and apron and find you work as a nursery maid." My skin did prickle, but if that was from something other than the cold, I sure wasn't going to admit it to Roth. My stomach growled. There was no place to buy food near where Roth and I had camped, so we hadn't eaten since the previous noon. When I stared at the mine entrance, though, my stomach hurt less. Should I be worried about that? Roth watched me with his brows drawn down. I hunched my shoulders to ward off his stupid concern.

Something moved near the huts. A man crawled out, struggled to his feet, and staggered toward the mine entrance. He wasn't wearing a cloak, so it was easy to see how thin he was. A woman poked her head out of another hut, and the bundle of rags at the gate straightened out and turned into a girl about my age.

"Almost time," the guard called. "Don't get pushy. We'll let you in."

Another guard appeared inside the gate, unlocked it, and shoved it ajar. The girl and the thin man flashed inside before the gate was all the way open. More people came out of the huts, all of them looking weak and dazed, and all of them heading straight for the mines like kids eager for their Name Day treats. My empty stomach flipped over.

"Finders?" I murmured.

Roth nodded.

So Roth had been right after all. This was the heart stone mine. How long before Mum grew sick enough to look like these pitiful people? If I touched enough heart stones, would I be like them?

I scanned each woman. Was that one Mum? No. Too short. That one? Too broad-shouldered. Roth and I had waited an extra day to be sure Mum had time to be brought here, so where was she?

"Move!" The guard snapped his fingers once at the dog. It growled, and when the Finders shuffled faster, the guard laughed. Fury spurted through me, lodging in my clenched fists. The Finders were already hurrying into the mines as fast as their shaking legs would carry them. When the last of them vanished, the gate clanged shut.

"Did you see Mum?" I asked frantically.

"No." Roth sounded like he had to squeeze the word out.

I started to push through the bushes, but Roth grabbed my ankle and pulled me backward through the snow, twigs tugging at my hair and snow sliding up my shirt. I scrambled up to face him.

"We need to get into that mine!" I said. A little voice in my head cried, Yes! I turned back toward the mine.

Roth spun me around by my shoulder. "You're not going in there ever, you hear me?"

"But Mum—"

"Mum isn't there, but the guard and the dog are. We're no good to Mum if we get caught."

"But where is she?"

He was silent for a long moment. "I don't know."

I slammed the heel of my hand into his chest. "You're useless! At least searching the mine is an idea."

"A bad one." Roth started down the back side of the hill.

I skidded after him. "Then what are we going to do?"

"Shut up, Cade. I'm thinking."

I tried to shut up, but I couldn't. "Why would they keep Mum out of the mine?"

"Maybe they thought it would be bad for her," Roth said. "The miners are supposed to take care of the Finders."

"They didn't have cloaks, and they were twig thin. That didn't look like taking care to me," I said.

Roth walked silently, wrinkling the space between his eyebrows. "Me either," he finally said.

Anger churned hot in my guts. Miners got rich from those heart stones. I'd seen their houses in the city. So how come Finders lived in huts in the cold? How could that be right?

When we reached the road leading to the mines, I turned left.

Roth yanked on my arm. "Where do you think you're going?"

Tricky gods, I was going toward the mines. "Those Finders were in bad shape, Roth. Don't you think we should try to free them?" It was an excuse, but it was also true.

"You saw them," Roth said. "I'm not sure they'd come with us." He hauled me the other way. I looked back, tried to look away, looked back again. The air felt warmer in that direction.

We got to the place where the mine road entered the main one running to and from Cor City. Roth stopped.

"Now what?" I said.

"I promised Mum I'd get you out of the city," Roth said.

"And you did, but now we need to figure out where Mum is and look for her. Who'd know where else the miners put Finders?"

Roth rubbed his scruffy beard. I knew it itched, but my guess was some girl had said she liked beards, and he figured he'd grow one rather than try to talk to her. Girls always smiled at Roth, and it always turned him into a stuttering idiot.

"Well," he said slowly, "there are laws about Finders, but I don't know all the ins and outs."

"That lawyer you worked for!" I cried. "You think we should ask him?"

He nodded. "I'll go on my own, though. That neighborhood is dangerous for you if someone recognizes us. People make money turning Finders in. I think Duval is trustworthy, but I don't like to take a chance."

"I'm going," I said.

He scowled down at me.

"Or you can leave me here." I gestured back along the rutted road to the mines. "I'm sure I can find something to do."

"You think this is funny?" Roth shook my arm hard.

"I think we should stop wasting time."

He shifted from one foot to the other, then blew out his breath. "In the name of all eight gods, what are brothers for anyway? All right. Come on."

We turned toward Cor City and started walking.

#

Duval's house was on Long Street, not far from the shrine where Mum was arrested. Roth and I slunk toward it with our hoods up. It felt like everyone was watching us. My stomach was so tight, I was almost glad I hadn't eaten. When Roth opened Duval's door, I hustled in.

Books filled floor-to-ceiling shelves on two walls. Behind a big desk, a gray-haired man raised his gaze from the parchment he was writing on. His hand jerked, spattering ink across the page.

"Roth!" He looked down at the spoiled page, swore once, and set his quill aside. When he rose to rush toward us, I thought he was going to shake Roth's hand, but instead he went to the door and locked it.

My breath stopped. I spun looking for another way out. Roth lunged for a doorway on the room's other side.

"Wait! Wait!" Duval said. "I'm not going to hurt you. It's just that Beam has been around looking for you. Roth, wait."

Roth halted, but he shoved me toward the doorway.

"I heard what happened to your mother," Duval said. "And when you didn't turn up for work, I thought you'd fled. I take it at least one of you has reason to fear being seized by the miners?"

"Of course not." Roth looked his boss straight in the eye.

I stared at my shoes so Duval wouldn't see my face. I'd never heard Roth lie outright before.

"We're looking for our mother," Roth said, "and she's not at the heart stone mine. Do you know where else she might be?"

Duval's sharp gray eyes had gone from Roth to me and then swept over our carry bags and wet, muddy clothes. He nudged a bench with his foot. "Sit down, both of you, while I get you something to eat. You both look ready to fall over."

My stomach growled, but Roth didn't move, so neither did I.

"Roth, you know me," Duval said. "I swear I won't hurt you."

After a moment, Roth nodded, and I moved out of the doorway and collapsed onto the bench. Duval vanished into the back of the house. Roth wandered to a smaller desk and played with the pen wiper that was the only thing on it. I recognized it as the one Mum had made him for his sixteenth Name Day. She got all teary remembering the day she and Dad decided their first baby was healthy enough to live and told everyone he was "Roth." He moved to the shelves and ran his finger along the leather spines of a row of books.

"Maybe when we get wherever we go, you can apprentice to another lawyer," I said.

"Maybe," Roth said, but I could tell he didn't believe it.

Duval came back into the room with a platter of cold chicken. I swallowed the drool trying to leak out the corners of my mouth. "I sent my housekeeper out on an errand, so you're safe."

Duval put the platter on the bench, and Roth sat on its other side. We both tore into the food while Duval went to sit behind his desk again. He rested his clasped hands on it, leaned toward us, and spoke low.

"You asked where else Finders might be, and the answer is here in town. The price of heart stones is shooting sky high, and there are rumors that some of the stones being sold are false. The miners are worried about fakes getting into their goods. The jewelers too for that matter. So the miners have Finders in town checking their shipments, and they're also making good money renting Finders out to jewelers."

My hand convulsed on the bone I was holding. "Renting Finders out? You're talking about people, which means no one owns them, so they can't be rented out." My voice rose with each word.

Duval lifted his hands like he was helpless or something even though he was a lawyer and lived in a big house. "I don't make the laws. Governor Barth and his council do, and the law says miners control the fate of Finders."

Of course it did. Governor Barth was head of the miners' syndicate.

"Slavery is illegal in Midland." I shook Roth's hand off my arm. "No one has the right to treat Finders like they're being treated at that mine."

"They have the right," Duval said soberly. "Whether it's a just thing to do is a different matter."

I shoved a hunk of meat between my teeth and tore it apart.

The door handle rattled. We all looked toward it. Someone knocked.

"Duval?" a man said. "You in there?"

"He has an appointment," Duval whispered.

The man pounded louder. "Duval?"

Roth's eyes met mine. I jerked my head a finger-width toward the door and raised an eyebrow. Was this really just a client and not a Watchman that Duval had sent for when he was out of our sight?

"Coming!" Duval called, then turned to us. "Hide in the kitchen. I'll get rid of him." He rose.

I grabbed my carry bag and the platter of chicken, then hurried after Roth down a dark hall and into a kitchen with a fireplace and some half-peeled potatoes on the table.

From Duval's office came the raised voice of the man who'd been knocking. "I hope I didn't make this trip for nothing."

"Roth?" My heart sped up.

Grim-faced, he nodded toward the back door. "Let's go."

I dumped the rest of the chicken into my bag and followed him out into the yard. He headed straight for the gate, and then we ran along an alley between high wooden fences. We didn't slow until we came out into a lane, where running would only make everyone turn to look. He jerked my hood over my head and raised his own. We walked along, breathing hard.

"What now?" I puffed. "And don't say we have to leave."

He was silent for a moment. "Looking for her could take a while. So first, we need a place to live where no one knows us."

"Yes!" I pounded his back.

"And since we don't have a lot of money, we'll need work," Roth said, "preferably work that lets us hear about jewelers or miners using Finders to check their heart stones."

"And we won't quit until we find her, right?" I said.

He nodded. "We won't quit until we find her."

4. DELIVERIES

The road turns. Will you?—Geat, the gatekeeper god
    Two weeks later, we'd seen no sign of Mum. I was getting more and more worried, and I could see Roth was too. All we could do was work at our new jobs delivering stuff to rich houses because that was where we could hear about Finders in town, and because we had to eat.

Where was she? I wondered, gulping a drink in the kitchen of today's fancy place.

"Why are you just standing there, boy?" The cook snapped his fingers like I was supposed to jump. "What kind of lazy louts is Elgar hiring these days? I don't see the flour. Go fetch it."

The girl who'd given me the water grabbed the cup and scuttled back to scrubbing pots. The kitchen smelled of cinnamon cakes like Mum always made for New Year. I used a handful of my shirt to wipe away the sweat itching under my chin and inhaled one more whiff. Then I strolled to the door, slowly enough to show the reptile cook that I didn't care about him but fast enough so he wouldn't charge after me and whack me one. Of course, he could still complain to Foreman Elgar, and then I'd be out of a job and out of a chance to look for Mum. I sped up.

"Bone idle," the cook said with a sneer I could hear.

"Tin pot tyrant," I muttered as I stepped out into the yard.

I spoke softly, but as the words trickled out, Elgar trudged into the yard with the sack of flour on his shoulder. Sweat spread out under his armpits, and the sour stink of him killed the cinnamon lingering in my nose. He narrowed his eyes.

"Mind your mouth," he said.

You didn't get to be a foreman if you couldn't hold your tongue, a skill Elgar was set on passing along to me. I couldn't blame him. Elgar had eight kids, and you had to look out for your family.

Which was why it ate at your guts if you'd brought home a stone that drove your mum mad and cost your brother his normal life. The more I thought about that night, the more it seemed that none of this would have happened if I hadn't been so stupid. I should have known what the stone was and never brought it near my house.

I'll fix it, I vowed. Once Mum was free she'd be all right, and Roth could go back to lawyering and figuring out how to talk to girls.

I went around to the front courtyard. The only thing left in our cart was a barrel of wine. I lowered the ramp on the back and considered trying to roll the barrel into the house on my own, but it weighed more than I did. If it got away from me, it would probably punch a hole in a wall. I leaned against the cart to wait for Elgar.

Sweat trickled between my shoulder blades. The weather had turned hotter than even old folks remembered it ever being before New Year. The granny who lived near me and Roth said it was because the calendar was about to turn to 4000. Something about all those zeroes in a row sparked wild ideas in her head, so she and her fellow crazies were all enjoying themselves thinking up worse and worse things to happen.

Elgar came around the corner of the house. "Get into the cart." He pointed to the wine barrel. "Roll it toward me."

I moved to the foot of the ramp, but before I could climb up, shouts erupted from the house. "Thief! Thief!"

I spun to see a man race out the front door, looking back over his shoulder.

"Stop him, Cade!" Elgar cried.

Like a fool looking to get pounded, I flung myself in front of the thief. He crashed into me, slamming my shoulder into the ground. Dust puffed into my mouth and eyes, but I kicked and rolled and wound up on top. I raised my fist to make sure he stayed down. Before I could hit him though, his eyelids fluttered and fell shut. Now that I had a good look, I saw he was only a few years older than me, with brown hair and wide cheekbones. I let my arm fall.

"Good job." A manservant dragged me aside, while a second servant seized the thief's arm and pulled him to his feet. The servant who'd grabbed me slapped the kid across the face. The other servant held him, or he would have fallen, but blood dripped from a cut on the side of his mouth.

"Don't." I tried to hold the slapping servant's elbow, but he shook me off.

The household steward ran into the courtyard, his shiny shoes clattering on the cobblestones like horse's hooves. "Search him."

One of the servants held the slumping kid while the other pulled a knife from the boy's belt sheath and then emptied his pockets of a penny, a greasy cloth that had probably wrapped the kid's lunch, and a bit of yarn tied to a string. I used to feed stray cats at Master Joff's stables, and I recognized that last thing as a cat toy. The servant showed each thing to the steward, who shook his head. The servant stuck the knife and cloth in his own belt and tossed the string into the dust. The penny vanished.

"Turn him over to the Governor's Guard," the steward said.

"No!" The kid's head jerked up. White showed all around the edges of his eyes, like it did with horses' eyes when they were scared. He struggled feebly while the servants hauled him toward the gates.

I flashed onto a vision of Watchman Beam dragging Mum away, and I blocked their path like I should have done with Mum. "Why are you having him arrested?" My voice was shaking. "He didn't take anything."

Elgar grabbed my arm and yanked me out of the way.

"He was in the house where he had no right to be." The steward hurried after the boy, apparently not trusting the other servants to be mean enough on their own. "Put that wine in the buttery off the heartroom," he ordered as he passed us.

"Get in the cart." Elgar shoved me toward it.

I stared at the long scuff marks the boy's toes had left in the dirt. The kid's cat better be able to fend for itself because no one was coming home to do it. My chest heaved like I'd run a mile.

Elgar squeezed my arm. "Not our business," he said gruffly.

I made my fists unclench. Roth would kick my backside if I tangled with the Watch even if I didn't get myself arrested. And if I did, I couldn't keep hunting for Mum.

I climbed into the cart and got behind the barrel. I was doing the right thing.

"Roll it toward me," Elgar said.

I spread my hands on the rough wood of the barrel and shoved hard.

"Slowly!" Elgar said.

We eased it to the ground and rolled it into the wide front hallway. It rumbled on the stone floor, the noise bouncing off the walls. We headed toward the hallway's end and the huge, square room in the center of the house.

The moment I stepped through the doorway, my body twanged like a plucked fiddle string. Big tables had been set up all around the room, ready for this house's New Year party. But the only place that interested me was the altar that stood like they always did in the room's center. A maid in a cap and striped apron tweaked at the altar flowers. They were nice, but the jeweled lockbox in the altar's middle seemed to glow, hauling at me like a hooked trout.

It was the first time I'd been in the same room with a heart stone since I put the triangular one in Mum's hand.

Maybe the boy had meant to steal it but failed at thieving. That should make me feel better about tackling him, but it was hard to tell with the stone's hum zooming up and down my spine.

I turned my back on it. "Where?" I forced the word out.

Elgar glanced around, then nodded at a leather curtain. We rolled the barrel that way, and Elgar shouldered the curtain aside to show an alcove where food would be set out to be served at the party. A door at its back would lead to the kitchen. All we had to do was heave our barrel up into the waiting rack.

We maneuvered our barrel as close as we could, got our hands under it, and counted to three. Elgar's knees popped, and his face turned purple. We shoved the thing into place. It bounced off the other barrel and rolled back toward us. I imagined myself squished to jelly oozing all over the floor. Both of us braced our hands on it and put our backs to the wall. The barrel rocked, then thunked into place.

Elgar blew out whatever air he still had in his lungs, while I slumped against the wall beside him. The buzzing in my chest had stopped, and I no longer had to fight the urge to creep toward the altar. The heart stone couldn't be very big if a leather curtain cut off the feel of it.

I heard the steward babbling orders, so he was back from siccing the Watch on that scared boy I wasn't thinking about. Elgar pushed the curtain aside. I tensed, ready to resist the heart stone's pull.

I needn't have bothered. The leather curtain had nothing to do with how I felt. The stone wasn't there any more. I halted and stared at the altar.

The maid was gone, but the steward was there, bossing the servant who'd come back with him. "What were you doing to let that boy get so close? You were lucky he didn't take anything. He shouldn't have been here."

The servant flushed red and flexed his hand on the hilt of his belt knife. My guess was he was imagining a neat hole in the steward's back.

The steward lifted a chain of keys from his belt and inserted a tiny one in the clasp of the box. He lifted the lid to show a gleaming red stone. I sucked in air. It was the right color, but it wasn't the heart stone that had been there a short while ago.

This was bad. This was trouble. Heart stones always cost a fortune, and Roth's lawyer boss, Duval, had told the truth when he said that right now they sold for triple that. Our granny neighbor and her friends weren't the only ones saying that when the calendar changed, there'd be trouble. They also said the stones would protect a household from the coming plague and fire, and not just heal sickness the way they always did. Even if this house's owner didn't believe the fire and plague stuff, he impressed his friends and rivals by being able to afford a stone.

If someone found out the real stone was gone, maybe the boy wouldn't be blamed. After all, they'd found nothing on him. That left two possible patsies: Elgar and me. I swallowed hard.

The steward relocked the box. His gaze caught on us. "Are you two finished?"

"Yes, sir," Elgar said.

"Then be on your way." The steward jerked his head toward the hallway.

I followed Elgar out to the yard. I should warn him the house had been robbed, but if I did that, how would I explain what I knew about the stones? Maybe I could quit working for Elgar, and the Watch wouldn't know where to find me. Had I told Elgar where I lived? I thought I had. Not the street, but the Sig's Alley neighborhood. He'd wanted to know if I lived close enough to get to his warehouse good and early. Would Roth and I have to move again? Tricky gods! Would I have to tell Roth? Maybe no one would notice the stone was missing.

"Cade?" Elgar stood with one hand on the cart handle and the other holding out three hapennies. "You're done for the day. I'll take the cart back by myself."

I frowned. He was letting me go now so he could pay me less. I opened my mouth to protest.

A ripple of power ran across my back like a creature with long toenails.

I whirled around. The maid from the heartroom was crossing the courtyard, carrying a market basket over her arm. It wasn't the boy after all! The maid had swapped out the stones and was carrying the real one away right under our noses.

I snatched the coins from Elgar's hand.

"Be on time tomorrow," he called as I scrambled away.

"I'll be there," I flung over my shoulder and pelted out the gate after her.

5. THE THIEF

A hero shields a child.—Sceld, the hero god

I turned right, the way the girl had. People were trailing along, drooping from the heat, but she was nowhere in sight. The house we'd been delivering to sat on Outer Circle Road, one of the two wide streets where city walls had once stood but which were now lined by rich folks' houses. She must have ducked into one of the streets that ran like spokes to the old temple market.

I skidded to a halt at the first corner but didn't see her. Two little girls of maybe five or six had chalked a hopscotch grid on the road. One of them threw a pebble, jumped along the squares, and stopped to spit at a young man who walked across it in front of her.

Nice. I crossed her off the list of people I'd let in my house and swerved toward the other tyke. "Did a maid with a market basket go down this lane?"

She pursed her sweet mouth and stuck out a grimy paw. "Pay me to tell you, you pustulant pig."

I frowned. "What does pustulant mean?"

She opened and closed her mouth, then said, "It means you!" She poked my belly. "Gimme a penny."

"What are you, some sort of apprentice highwayman?"

Her friend muscled between us, her head not far above my belt. Snot had gathered under her button nose, and heat rash bloomed on her arms. "She went that way." She pointed farther along the Outer Circle.

I took three steps in that direction, then spun and caught them gleefully prancing like evil kittens.

"Thank you!" I backed up and raced down the lane they hadn't pointed to. Behind me, one of the little darlings said a bad word.

A faint hum vibrated in my chest, growing stronger as I sped toward the market, dodging people heading home to their supper. I glanced both ways down the Inner Circle when I crossed it, but didn't see the girl. I ran another few yards, then realized the whisper of the stone was gone.

I turned back to the Inner Circle, looked both ways, and followed the trembling air leading right. People slunk along between the garden walls lining the street. There was a girl carrying a basket, but her blond hair hung down her back, and no apron covered her pink dress, so I ran past her. The tingle of the stone grew stronger, then faded just as I realized what I'd glimpsed from the corner of my eye. The girl's basket overflowed with a striped maid's apron.

I spun and ran back. When an older woman and little boy glanced my way, I tried to look harmless. "There you are!" I cried. "You should have waited for me to carry your basket." I grabbed for the handle.

She yanked it away and opened her mouth to scream.

I crowded in and spoke low. "Make a scene, and I'll tell everyone what's in that basket." I braced myself to run if she went ahead and yelled because being found near a heart stone had to be much worse for me than for her even though she'd stolen it.

She darted looks to both sides, saw how people had slowed to poke their noses in our direction, and swallowed whatever noise she'd been going to make. When I reached for the basket again, she backed into a niche in a garden wall, tucking her prize behind her.

"Smile." She looked over my head at passers-by. "Look friendly."

I bared my teeth at her. After a moment, the footsteps behind me moved on.

"What do you want?" she said. Her face was long and narrow, with bright blue eyes and a dusting of pale freckles.

"Give me the heart stone you stole from that house." At the thought of touching a heart stone, a little thrill ran through me, reminding me that was a bad idea. "No. Wait. Put it back where you got it."

She gave a shaky laugh. "What makes you think I have a heart stone?"

I hesitated. "I saw you take it."

"You did not," she said. "You couldn't have because you—because I didn't."

"Liar. It's in there right now."

She pushed me away with feeble little shoves. I was used to girls who were bigger versions of the two hellions playing hopscotch, but this one hadn't worked hard enough to build muscles. Of course not. She was a thief, not a maid.

"They'll make that boy pay for your theft," I said.

At the mention of the boy, her face tightened. "It wasn't theft. That stone doesn't belong to them."

"They think it does, and when they find out it's missing, what happens to him?"

"It's a little late to ask that when you're the one who knocked him down."

Feeble she might be, but that hurt like she'd punched me in the stomach. Sharp teeth gnawed at my gut when I remembered how I'd put Mum in the law's hands. The thought of the boy too winding up in jail because of me made them take a big bite.

"I know you took it." I grabbed for the basket again.

She was enough taller than me that she just lifted it out of my reach. "How? How do you know that?" She drew a noisy breath. "You're like Jem. You're a Finder, aren't you?"

"A Finder?" I nearly choked myself forcing out a laugh. "Don't be stupid."

"Now who's lying?"

I needed to talk to her some place with fewer passers-by than the Inner Circle. I grabbed her hand and towed her toward the next lane. At its end, I could see the spire of the ruined city temple rising over the people milling around the market.

"Let me go." She twisted her hand in mine.

"Just as soon as you say you'll take that stone back." I was getting more and more worried. Even if I hauled her back to that house, I couldn't go in, so I couldn't be sure she'd return the stone. I had to persuade her it was the right thing to do for the good of that scared kid she called Jem. Anyone could see she had a soft spot for him. I dragged her along, looking for an empty side street.

Her hand slipped out my sweaty grip just as a herd of pigs swept around the corner from the market and came trotting toward us. At their rear, a butcher's boy swung a stick to keep them moving.

"Out of the way," he shouted.

The girl flung herself to the other side of the lane. I grabbed for her, but the lead pig rammed my legs and bounced off to run between us, followed by every one of his stinking, squealing friends. The herd parted not quite far enough to run around me. Pigs knocked me forward, back, and sideways, whirling me like a top. I staggered and struggled to keep my feet. Then as the boy drove the last one past, I slid in pig droppings and sat down with a jolt that made my teeth skin the edges of my tongue. Thank the gods the only thing I landed in was dirt.

"Fool," the boy called over his shoulder. "Watch where you're going."

Sucking blood, I leapt to my feet, but the girl had vanished. Curse it!

Pustulant pigs blocked the way we'd come, so the girl must have headed for the market. I ran down the lane to where booths sprawled in a circle around the old temple. It stood at the center of Cor City, just like Cor City stood at the center of Midland, and Midland stood at the center of the world. A couple of hundred years ago, it had probably been impressive, but it was a wreck now, its spire leaning like it was trying to peek in the upstairs window of a boarding house.

I dodged through the crowd. "Gods," I prayed, "I'm at your temple. How about a little guidance?"

Ahead, I glimpsed a woman dressed in pink ducking between the shoppers. I jumped toward her, but a thin-as-hunger man stepped in front of me, holding up something wrapped in coarse, brown cloth. "The world's going sour, young man."

"Can't argue with that." I tried to go around him, but he sidestepped.

"Maybe you'd like some protection?" Eyes flicking side to side, he slid the cloth open for an instant and showed me a red stone. I flinched, but from fear, not the touch of a heart stone. Was everyone tossing fake stones around today? If this guy was a beggar, the thing he was begging for was trouble.

"I haven't any money." I tried again to get around him, but again he blocked my path.

"It's meant for you, young man." He pushed his sweat-slicked face close to mine, swaying like a boat in a storm. He smelled sour, like ale gone bad. His eyelids drooped, and he fell into me.

I steadied him with a hand on his elbow. "You want to sit down?" I looked around for a place to dump him.

He blinked. "If you don't take it, don't blame me for what happens." He moved aside. "Go."

"You sure you're all right?"

He waved me off.

I looked over my shoulder until the crowd hid him. Then I circled the rest of the market half-a-dozen times, but too late. If the girl had ever been there, she was gone.

6. THE JEWELERS

To see, do more than look.—Myst, the shapeshifter god

Searching for the girl had made me so late that I ran all the way to Sig's Alley, where we'd rented a place with a few sticks of furniture. Our dad had grown up in Sig's Alley, and it wasn't the worst part of the city, but it was crummier than Sceld's Gate, where we lived before. I tore up the lane and through our door.

"Where have you been?" Roth thumped a plate onto the rickety table and put his hands on his hips. Our one-room house was small enough that we had to roll the sleeping pallets up during the day if we wanted to walk around the table. So there wasn't much room ever, and right now, Roth filled it. "You're supposed to go to the market and come straight home after work," he said.

"The market was crowded." I'd been wondering if I should tell him about the girl and the stolen heart stone and Jem the Finder, but he'd just reminded me why that was a bad idea. I kept the table between us and put down the bread and sausage I'd bought.

Roth grabbed a knife and divided the food, setting some aside for the next day and shoving half the rest toward me. "Hurry up and eat. We're going out."

My breath caught. "You heard of another Finder?" I dropped onto my stool, slapped sausage onto bread, and crammed it in my mouth.

"Another Finder at a jeweler's shop. Don't get your hopes up. It may turn out like the other three."

I gobbled my supper without tasting it. I was chewing the last of it when Roth lifted the loose floorboard and took out the little bag holding Dad's wedding ring.

"You ready?" Roth went out the door without waiting for my answer.

Rubbing my greasy hands on my trousers, I followed. As soon as I was outside, a chill slid down my back and goose bumps popped out on my arms. Clouds rolled across the sky, blocking the emerging stars. It had been clear and hot when I got home. I was glad of the cooler air but startled by how fast it had come in.

Roth headed along the row of connected houses. The baby next door was screaming, but the couple in the second house were shouting loudly enough to nearly drown it out. On a stool outside the third door sat the old lady all the neighbors called Granny. Her white hair puffed around her head like dandelion fluff.

"Good evening, boys." She raised her voice over the usual Sig's Alley noise. "I told you the weather would change." She rubbed the shoulder that twinged when it rained. "The calendar's knocking the world out of balance. Now there'll be storms and earthquakes and plagues." She smiled, showing the gaps where three of her teeth used to be. If she hadn't been so obviously enjoying herself, her predictions would have sounded scarier. "That's what the old books say. There's sickness in town, you know."

"Folks are always sick when it's hot," I said.

"Don't believe me then. You'll see." She shivered and hugged herself.

"You need help to go inside?" Roth asked.

"Go on," she said. "I'm not so old I can't manage."

"She's right about the sickness," Roth said as he strode off. "My foreman fired a man today because he collapsed and couldn't work. It didn't matter that the man has a wife and new baby."

"You think plague and flood and stuff really will happen next week?" I asked. "Is it really in books?"

"I don't know," he said. "I never spent much time on misty things like prophecies."

We hurried through the deepening dark. At length, Roth steered us into a street of shops that a blind man would know sold expensive goods because the road was paved. "It's somewhere along here," he said. Shutters covered all the windows, but when we got up close, we could make out the shop signs even in the dark. We passed a silversmith, a silk merchant, and a boot maker.

"There," I said. The sign showed the gold rose symbol of the jewelers' syndicate and read, *Olstaff. Fine Jewelry.* We stopped outside. My breath wheezed like a leaky bellows. I quieted it, then raised my fist to knock.

Roth put his hand on my arm. "Check first."

"I don't have to," I said. "If they had a heart stone in there, I'd know."

Roth hung onto me for half a moment, then let go. I knocked. We waited long enough that even Roth was jiggling his leg. I knocked again.

"I'm coming," said an irritated voice. The door cracked open, and a young man peered out. Not Olstaff, of course, but the apprentice who slept over the shop. He was barefoot and his hair stood up on one side, so he'd probably been in bed when he heard us.

"We're closed," he said. "Come back during the day." He started to shut the door, but Roth stuck his foot in the gap.

"We've run into some trouble and need to sell this right away." Roth held up Dad's ring.

"I can't do anything now." The apprentice nudged Roth's toe with his bare one. "Come back tomorrow."

Roth shoved the ring under the apprentice's nose. "We can't wait. If you won't help, we'll go elsewhere."

The apprentice squinted at the ring, cocking his head. We'd been surprised the first time a jeweler perked up at the sight of Dad's ring, but they always did. Mum had it from her father who won it in a card game. If I could pick one of my dead grandparents to meet, he'd be the one. The ring's green stone nested like an egg in a circle of twisted golden metal.

The apprentice chewed his lower lip, then opened the door. We went in and waited while he lit a lantern and set it on the counter. The shop looked like the other three we'd been in. No jewelry was in sight, but locked boxes sat on shelves. Narrow stairs rose to the apprentice's loft. A door at the back would open into the yard, which was where I needed to be, because that's where Olstaff would keep his Finder. I hoped.

The apprentice spread a soft cloth on the counter and flicked a finger toward it. When Roth laid the ring on the cloth, the apprentice moved the lantern closer and bent over the ring.

Roth glanced my way and nodded.

I shifted from foot to foot and hugged my belly. "Can I use your privy?" I took a step toward the back door.

"No." Without looking away from the ring, the apprentice groped under the counter and pulled out a lens. He held it over the ring.

"Please. I really have to go." I moaned. "The fish we had for supper must have been bad." I hunched over and edged closer to the back door.

"Let him use it." Roth reached for the ring. "Otherwise, we have to leave."

The apprentice put his hand over the ring and frowned at me. "All right, but don't dawdle."

I lifted the bar from the door and shoved out into the high-walled yard. The air nipped my ears, and in the distance, lightning flashed.

The privy was there, of course, but so was a lean-to. The other lean-to we'd found was just barred on the outside, so I could open it, but this one was locked. I rapped on the door, then put my ear against it. Something rustled. Did the noise come from inside or was it just a rat creeping through the high grass by the fence?

Thunder rolled, then vibrated in my chest like an echo.

"Anyone there?" I asked softly.

No answer.

The lean-to's only window was barred and a yard over my head. I found a bucket of ashes in the privy, dumped the ashes down the hole, and turned the bucket over to stand on. I still wasn't high enough to reach the bars, much less see in. When I bent my knees and jumped, the bucket clattered away with a noise like a collapsing wood pile, but I managed to grab the bars. For a moment, I dangled. You didn't hear that, I thought to the apprentice. The bars creaked in the rotting wood frame as I hauled myself up and peeked in. The tiny room was dark, so I hooked my elbows around the bars and waited. When lightning flashed again, I glimpsed a frayed pallet with no one on it, and no blankets or clothes or any other sign someone lived there.

The window cracked a warning, then ripped loose in a hail of splinters. I smashed to the ground, pain battering my shoulder and hip.

The door burst open, and the apprentice ran out with Roth right behind him. The apprentice ran to the privy, but Roth turned to me. I could see him scanning for broken bones even from the doorway. I hastily dropped the bars I was still holding and was pushing myself to my knees when the apprentice came out of the privy and saw me. He goggled at the ruined window.

"What did you do?" he asked.

"Nothing. Someone threw a rock at the window and knocked it loose, and I was just running over here to see." I climbed the rest of the way to my feet. "I tripped."

He snorted. "Do you think I'm a fool? There's damage here." He waved at the wreckage.

Roth darted up next to me and gave my arm a squeeze that said *Shut up, Cade*. "Damage?" Roth said. "What does it matter? That shack is such a wreck I can't believe you ever had a Finder anyway."

"Of course we did," the apprentice said, affronted. "We did until a week ago when the miners pumped the rent up too high. But it doesn't matter." He pointed to me. "The kid was fooling around where he shouldn't have been, and he broke the window. I'm keeping that ring to make sure you come back and pay for it."

I started to protest, but Roth squeezed my arm again and hurried me past the apprentice and through the shop door. As soon as we were inside, Roth whirled to slam and bar the door in the face of the open-mouthed apprentice. I snatched Dad's ring from the counter as we raced past on our way to the street. From out front, I could barely hear the apprentice pounding on the door and shouting.

We hot-footed away, walking, but fast enough that we were both breathing hard, me cursing under my breath. "Sorry about all the noise I made," I said.

"It's all right." Roth wiped his hand down his face and then went on talking as if to himself. "We're just searching. And we're really not wrecking property. That window was rotten."

"So were they," I said. "They shouldn't be 'renting' people. They're just using Finders to get rich. The miners would be sorry if they ever tried to rent me out, I'll tell you that."

Roth gave a short laugh. "True enough. They'd have to pay the jewelers to let you work for them."

We walked on for a while before I said, "Roth, I know you don't want to hear this, but we have to start looking in miners' houses."

"Halt," a man barked.

Tricky gods. My heart had just stopped kicking against my ribs, and now it started going again. Two Watchmen were coming toward us, the taller one carrying a lantern. Lit from below, their faces were all jaw and eyes circled in black like someone had socked them. The taller one held the lantern up to get a look at us. I blinked in the light.

"What are you two doing out after curfew?" the taller one said.

"Curfew?" I said.

Roth squeezed my arm in that same shut-up-Cade way.

"No one's allowed out after dark without a permit," the taller one said. "It was decreed today after Governor Barth learned someone stole a heart stone last week."

Last week? Not the one the girl thief took today then, though I'd bet she strolled off with it in her basket too.

"We're sorry," Roth said. "We didn't know."

"That's no excuse," the taller Watchman said. "We should arrest you."

Roth's hand convulsed on my arm. My heart flipped over in my chest.

Lightning flashed. I cut my eyes to one side, then the other. No alley escape route blinked into sight.

"We were working late." Roth's voice was tight. "We'll just hurry on home now."

"Only if I say you will." The taller Watchman stuck out his chin and strolled closer. He was enjoying himself.

The shorter Watchman cleared his throat. "It's a new decree. And we'd have to take them to the station. That's a long way."

Thunder cracked. A fat raindrop hit me on the head like a stone from a slingshot, followed by a handful more, and then it was like being under a waterfall. I was soaked to the skin before I could twitch.

Yelping, the shorter Watchman dove into the shelter of a doorway. Clearly torn, the taller one twisted toward him, then back to us. He reached for Roth.

Enough fooling around. I put both hands on the tall one's back and shoved. The Watchman stumbled forward and fell to his knees in the rain.

"Run!" I shouted, but Roth was already moving. When my legs couldn't keep up, he grabbed my arm and dragged me after him. We tore through the blinding rainfall, rounding one corner, and then another.

A man shouted behind us, but when I looked over my shoulder, I didn't see anyone. We ran for home, kicking up mud in the lanes melting underfoot. We burst into our house, and I slammed the door behind us.

Rain dripped off my nose. My skin itched where my clothes stuck to it. I shivered, colder than I'd been since the snow melted. I leaned against the door, my chest heaving. This had not been a good night so far, and if the Watch was hunting heart stone thieves, tomorrow might be worse. I straightened up. Maybe I should tell Roth about being at the house where today's stone was stolen.

I was just opening my mouth when Roth flung me back against the door and glared at me. "If you ever do anything that stupid again, I swear I'll lock you in the house." Hands on my shoulders, he leaned over me, close enough that I could smell the wet-dog scent of his rain-soaked clothes. I tried to draw my head back, but it was already pressed against the door. "For once in your life, could you please not do the first idiotic thing that pops into your head?"

"Was I supposed to let them arrest us?"

"They wouldn't have," Roth said. "They both just wanted out of the rain. I got us out of that jeweler's shop, and I'd have talked us out of the hands of the Watch too. Trust me to take care of trouble."

I snorted. "What do you think I do when there's trouble and you're not around?"

He froze. "Have you been in trouble?"

I hesitated. "No." I'd be hanged if I told him about the girl thief. He was likely to hook me to a leash and tie me to his belt.

Still scowling, he kicked off his mud-caked shoes, unbuttoned his soaked shirt, and turned away to hang it on its hook.

"Do you think they'll find us?" I asked.

"I'd never seen either of them before. Had you?"

"No."

"Then they don't work in this neighborhood, which means they don't know us and don't know where we live."

My icy fingers fumbled at my buttons. "So what do you think about what I said? Mum is probably in a miner's house checking the stone shipments. I know a house would be harder to search than a shop, but we need to figure out a way to do it."

He stood with his back to me and his hands on his dripping shirt. "Right. You should sneak into a miner's house. No. I'm not spitting on the law and lying my backside off and still losing everyone I love. You're not doing that." He set the basin on the table, poured water from the bucket, and flung a dirty dish into it. Water sloshed out onto the table.

"I went to the mine with you," I said. "That's at least as dangerous. And I go into miners' houses for work sometimes."

He looked up sharply. "Elgar's always with you, right? You're not taking chances?"

"Of course not," I said, wiping all thoughts of the girl thief out of my head in case they showed on my face.

"The mine was different. I had no choice about that because I couldn't leave you. I'm keeping an eye out when I work at miners' houses, and I checked on that one Finder who turned out to be an old man."

"I wish you'd set him loose. I would have."

"I told you, he wouldn't come." Roth's face was winter bleak.

I balled up my shirt and splatted it against the wall.

7. SHAN

It's only a joke!—Ras, the trickster god
In the dark, a heart stone pulsed like a hot coal. I couldn't take my eyes off it, but then Mum was there, on the other side of the stone. She lifted her pale face to me and stretched out a shaking hand. For me or the stone? She leaned forward, then fell and fell.

I started awake with a gasp. For a handful of galloping heartbeats, I didn't know where I was. Then I recognized the damp underside of our roof. Rain drummed on the wood tiles and dripped through at the edge, splashing into the bucket Roth had set there before we went to bed. Good thing too, because if he hadn't, rainwater would have spread across the floor and into our pallets.

Where are you, Mum?

Roth stirred, then sat up, but that was as far as he got. He'd tossed and turned in the night. His eyes were shadowed.

I scrambled to my feet and pulled on my still damp clothes. Then I grabbed my cloak from its hook, snatched up the bread and sausage we'd set aside for today, and pulled the door open. Rain wasn't so much falling as launching itself into the puddles.

"What's your hurry?" Roth lifted his hair off his ears. Mum would have been after him to let her cut it. "Stop letting in the cold."

"Elgar said to be early." I stepped outside, closing the door behind me. I was wet as a fish and muddy to the knee before I got to the first corner.

Elgar's warehouse squatted along a lane just off Ridge Road. I glanced that way but turned in the other direction. Yesterday, the girl thief hadn't just said I was a Finder. She'd said I was a Finder "like Jem." And that meant Jem was in trouble, and I was the one who'd put him there. I wanted to see if he was in as much trouble as I thought.

I cut across an alley and into a lane leading toward the largest houses in Cor. When I got to Inner Circle Road, I slipped along it until I could stand in a doorway and study Syndicate House, where the governor lived. It loomed above its courtyard gates, three stories tall, with red clay tile on the roof and real glass in the windows. This early, the front gates were closed, but the gate to the traders' jail was at the back. Break an ordinary law, and the Watch took you to one of their cells. Break one of the laws protecting the trade syndicates, and you wound up here in the custody of the Governor's Guards. I knew which one sounded worse to me. Folks called the Governor's Guards "Crows" for their black uniforms and called their jail the Crows' Hole. You got out of there only when the Syndicate council said so.

I crossed the road and splashed down the narrow walkway between Syndicate House and the one next door. Halfway down, a woman leaned against the governor's garden wall holding a sleeping child. When she saw me, she drew aside to let me pass. Rain dripped from her hood, but not enough to hide her scared face. Being near the Crows' Hole scared most people, so I couldn't imagine why she'd hang around, especially since the kid was whimpering and red-faced, really sick from the look of it.

I didn't have time to waste wondering about her, so I hurried on. From beyond the wall came the faint pull of a heart stone, which made sense, because Governor Barth was sure to have one. Maybe that was what the woman was after. She'd heard about the governor's stone, and she was trying to borrow some healing for the kid. She might be able to do it too. Governor Barth's stone must be huge for me to feel it at this distance and through more than one wall.

At the back of the house, two Crows pressed under the gate, but it wasn't wide enough to keep off all the rain. The shoulders of their cloaks were splotched, and drops rolled down their helmets. One of the Crows stood straight, like a man proving a little rain didn't bother him. The other curled in on himself, looking as miserable as I felt. I pulled my hood as far forward as it would go and sloshed up to the miserable one.

"Please, sir." I held up my breakfast bread, so he'd look at it rather than me. "It's bread for Jem, the boy you're holding. His mum sent it. Can I go in to give it to him?"

"Get out of here." The Crow nudged the bread away with the butt of his pike. "He'll eat what we give him."

"Oh, let him in." The other Crow laughed. "If he makes trouble, we'll just lock him up too."

"Don't be ridiculous." The miserable one prodded my shoulder. "Get away before I arrest you. Move!"

I moved. So they'd arrested Jem. Curse the miners anyway.

Back in the passage, the kid was awake and whining for a drink. His mother smiled and stroked his cheek. I gawked at how much better he was, but I was late for work and had to run. As I pelted along, I shoved bread in my mouth and chewed hard, trying to grind up my guilt about Jem. Eventually, I tore around a corner and down the lane to Elgar's place. At least my trip had warmed me up. It was going to be a punishing day, pushing carts through puddles and muck and rain until I went home again that night.

A cloaked and hooded figure stepped out from under an archway and blocked my path. I tried to dodge, but the person laid a gloved hand on my arm. I looked up to see the thin-faced girl who'd stolen the heart stone. Her freckles stood out against her pale face. Her blond hair wasn't dripping down her neck in rat-tails, so her hood was better oiled than mine.

"I have to talk to you," she said.

"You going to put that stone back? Maybe see to it that Jem is let out of jail?"

"I can't put the stone back. I need it."

"Then get away from me." I tried again to go around her, but she knotted her fingers in my cloak.

"Just for a moment. Please."

She was a polite thief. I'd give her that.

She drew me under the shelter of the arch. I edged out far enough to watch Elgar's doorway through the wash of rain. An empty cart stood in front of it. Elgar would be stomping around breathing fire for me to get there and load the cart.

"I'm Shan," she said. "I know you work for Elgar, but I don't know your name."

Did she think I was stupid? My heart was already jumping around in my chest just because she'd found me.

"What do you want?" I asked without looking at her. If I pretended she wasn't there, maybe she'd take the hint.

"I need to talk to you about heart stones."

Oh gods.

"I was right, wasn't I?" she said. "You're another Finder. You can tell which houses have the stones."

I snapped my gaze from Elgar's doorway to Shan's face. Rain had darkened her blue-gray hood to the same color as her eyes.

"You want me to help you steal heart stones?" I tried to laugh, but I sounded shaky even to me. "No. Find a safer way to make money. Maybe lion taming."

"This isn't about money," she said.

"A thief who doesn't want money? Right." I yanked myself out of her grip and folded my arms. "What is it about then?"

She hesitated. "You know about the calendar change? The trouble that's coming?"

"Is this a joke?"

She shook her head, and a drop of rain flew off her hood and hit me on the cheek. "People are getting sick. There were more than forty new cases of fever yesterday, and that's just among those who could afford to go to the healers. Two of those people died."

For a moment, I couldn't answer. That was a lot of fever-struck people. I pictured the woman with the sick kid at Syndicate House. Could Granny and the other crazies be right about the calendar change bringing disaster? It didn't matter. I couldn't let this girl involve me in her schemes. "Then those stolen stones will just bring you a bigger profit, won't they?"

Pink rose into her cheeks. "I told you, it's not about that! It's about keeping people safe. But we need your help."

I scanned her face. She looked to be only Roth's age, but her forehead was crinkled with what looked like honest worry. Of course, Roth looked that way a lot of the time too. "We?"

"I shouldn't have said that. I can't tell you about anyone else until I'm sure you're trustworthy."

"Sure *I'm* trustworthy? You're a thief!"

She shook her head, spattering me again. If I weren't already half-drowned, I'd have protested. "I already told you, I'm not a thief. Look. Maybe you don't believe the prophets, but are you willing to take a chance on the lives of everyone in Cor City? Isn't there anyone you care about here?"

I bit my lip. What if she was right? Roth and Mum lived here. But this girl was asking me to admit I was a Finder. How did I know she wouldn't sell me for a song?

"What are you doing about Jem?" I asked. "He's a human being, you know, though he is a Finder. He even has a cat."

She smiled, which annoyed me enough that I nearly left right then. "The cat's being taken care of," she said.

"Oh good. I'm sure that'll make Jem feel better when he's working in the mine. Do you know what it's like for Finders there? They live like animals in little huts with dogs and guards. But worse, they don't seem to care because the stones make them forget everything else. They're dying to go into the mine. And isn't that just great for the miners?"

She stretched herself taller and looked down her nose. "You don't know what you're talking about. The miners take care of Finders."

"I've been there, and nobody was taking care of Finders," I said. "The stones wash down into the rivers, sometimes even into the city water pipes. So the miners could get them there, enough for healers to use, but not enough to make miners rich, and they're as money mad as their Finders are stone mad. They say Finders are likely to hurt other people getting what they want, and maybe they do, but you know who does for sure? Miners."

She pulled her hood close, like she wanted to block her ears. Her face was red. "You think I don't care what happens to Jem? I do, but I need your help. What do I have to do to get it?"

"Jem's in the Crows' Hole. Get him loose," I said.

"How?"

"That's your problem. Don't you think you owe him?"

"Cade!" Elgar's voice boomed down the lane. "Is that you? Get over here!"

I'd never been glad to have Elgar shout at me before, but I wanted to be gone from this dangerous girl's company. I started away, but Shan grabbed my cloak.

"Cade!" she said urgently. "I'll find out what's happening with Jem. Meet me in the ruined temple after work, and I'll tell you what I learn and about the stones too."

I yanked my cloak free and ran toward Elgar.

"Cade!" Shan called after me. "Meet me, please. Everyone's good is at stake."

I dripped into Elgar's shop, shutting the door on the echoes of Shan's pleas. The place smelled of the fancy foodstuff stacked on the shelves around the walls and in the warehouse out back—spices, dried fruit, and wine, along with olive oil and more ordinary sacks of flour and sugar.

"About time." Elgar pointed to a pile of goods to be loaded. "I already had to send Dunnan out alone because Marc's down with this fever. I'd about decided you weren't going to show either."

"Is Marc very sick?" I asked.

"Sick enough to miss work for the first time in ten years." Elgar shuddered. "Covered with a pus-filled rash and out of his head." He nodded to the goods again.

As I heaved a sack of onions onto my shoulder, I worried about fever. Roth said someone who worked with him collapsed. And I'd seen not only the woman with the kid, but also the sick man selling heart stones and the hopscotch-playing girl with the rash on her arms. "Pustulant," she'd said. Maybe that meant "filled with pus," like Elgar said. Maybe she'd heard the word because someone at home had a rash squirting the revolting stuff.

So Shan had spoken truth about the fever. What about the other things she'd said?

#

In the market that evening, I tucked the bread and cheese I'd bought under my sopping cloak. The walls of the old temple rose above the rubble of the stone steps and columns that had once circled it. It had been built by the same people who built the shrines in Long Street and along the roads running from the market place to Cor City's eight old gates. Every kid in Cor went in there at some point, because their friends dared them. Roth claimed to have spent the night there, though I think he was teasing me because Mum would have killed him if he stayed out all night. Besides, if you were a normal kid, you'd never sleep in the temple because the place looked haunted with the monsters who lived down your privy at night. When I was seven, my knees had shaken, but I'd gone in anyway. The question was, should I ignore my shaking knees now and go in to meet Shan?

Of course, I shouldn't. I should go home. I was tired and wet and cold, and I didn't want to have to explain to Roth why I was late again. But Shan was checking on Jem, and she'd said she needed me to help keep people in Cor City safe. Since that included Roth and Mum, I couldn't just walk away.

I scaled the rock pile and squeezed past a heap of debris. Inside, rain washed through the half of the temple where the roof had caved in. I scanned the other half but didn't see Shan. I decided to wait a bit. I could always leave if she took too long to get there. At least, I'd be out of the rain.

I spread my cloak out to drip from the edge of a pitted stone altar, then walked around, looking the place over and trying to rub some heat into my arms. When I was little, I'd been in here only as long as it took to tear through it and burst out the other side. The temple had scared the snot out of me. From the corners of my eyes, I was sure I'd seen huge ghosts looming toward me, ready to grab hold.

Now I saw them again, only this time, I had to laugh. The walls were painted with larger-than-life pictures, faded and flaking in places. No ghosts, just pictures.

I moved closer to see what my ghosts were really doing rather than grabbing little kids and stuffing them into sacks. The first figure was a man who actually was carrying a sack. He had it over his shoulder and seemed to be fleeing. And no wonder. He looked over his shoulder at a row of broken and falling buildings. A jagged crack snaked across the ground behind him. Pieces of building cascaded into it, and so did a woman with her arms stretched to the sky.

I moved along in the direction the man was running. It didn't look like he was headed for safety. Ice pellets the size of my fist bounced off the ground in front of him. Another man stood under the ice storm with his shirt ripped off his shoulders and bunched around his waist. The picture was faded, but I could still see the fiery rash covering his body. A pile of rags at his feet turned out to be a woman who was either dead or giving a good imitation. Despite the ice, a wall of fire rose in the background.

My mouth was dry. I wanted my ghosts back. They were less terrifying.

A voice spoke in my ear. "This is why I wanted to meet you here."

I jumped and made a really girly noise.

Shan raised an eyebrow. "Sorry I scared you."

"I wasn't scared," I said. "What did you learn about Jem?"

"I talked to someone who works at Syndicate House," she said, "and Governor Barth won't hold a trial until after New Year, so Jem isn't going anywhere for at least that long."

"And then what?"

"Then if you help me, I think we can help him."

"Help you how?"

"Jem was our Finder. We need a new one. We need you."

"No."

"I thought you wanted to help Jem."

"I do, but—"

"Cade, listen." She pointed to the murals. "This is what happened a thousand years ago, the last time the calendar changed."

For a moment, my tongue flapped soundlessly. "That can't be right." I swallowed. "The gods are tricky, but they love us. Their jokes make us laugh, and laughing is good. But this—" I waved at the wall. "This wouldn't be a joke. They wouldn't do that to us."

"The world has energies of its own," Shan said, "the energy that makes grain grow and rain fall and wind blow. It's the energy in the heart stones too. When the calendar turns, the energy turns, and for a handful of days, the shock of it throws the world into chaos."

I stared at her profile. She was eyeing the murals again and twisting her hands so her gloves spiraled around her fingers. I didn't know if I believed what she was saying, but she sure did.

"Where are you getting all that about the energy?" I asked.

"From books left us by the prophets who designed the shrines and this temple." She turned to face me. "The ones who created a way to keep the changing energies from hurting us."

For a moment, silence filled the broken space. Even the rain held back.

"How?" I asked.

The rain pounded down again.

"Look here." Shan pointed to a picture of an altar set with a circle of red stones. Then she moved to the altar where I'd draped my cloak. "This temple is at the center of Cor, the center of the world. If we anchor it, it holds us safe in the energy storm." She ran her hand over the circle of hollows on the table.

"Anchor?" I echoed. Like the other dozen or so pits in the table, the one under her hand looked like a cup waiting to be filled.

"Heart stones have to be fitted into the table. We need three more, and we have only five days to get them." She looked me in the eye. "We need a Finder—"

"I'm not—"

"—to lead us to the stones in people's houses," Shan finished.

"Miners' houses?" I heard the sharpness in my own voice.

Shan frowned. "Anyone's house."

I could hardly breathe. Some of the houses would surely be miners'. I could go into them and look for Mum. All I had to do was admit to this stranger that I was a Finder.

"Please, Cade," Shan said. "You have a gift, indeed what scholars used to call The Gift. When you have a lot, you owe a lot."

Gift. Right.

"Besides," Shan went on, "if we do it right, the governor will be grateful enough to give us anything we want afterward, including Jem's freedom. You want to make up for putting him in jail, don't you?"

"My brother hears if I scratch a flea bite," I said. "I can't get out at night."

"We can't do it at night anyway. There's a curfew."

"But I work during the day."

"Every day?"

"Only if that's how often I want to eat."

She flushed. "I'll pay you what you'd otherwise make."

Tricky gods. I could not only look for Mum, but also get away from Elgar, which meant the Crows would have a harder time finding me. Of course, I'd be doing something crazy dangerous instead, but if Shan was right, it would be downright heroic to help her.

If Roth found out, he'd be so hot his hair would smoke.

"I'll do it," I said.

8. THIEVING

Beyond here, there's no turning back.—Geat, the gatekeeper god
The next morning, I stopped with my hand clutching the latch to Elgar's door. Wind hurled road grit against my cheek and rattled the latch under my hand. Wait. Maybe that was me shaking the latch. Was I really going to do this? What if Shan was just a thief after all?

I glanced toward the archway where we'd talked the day before and where she'd finally agreed to meet me this morning. She hadn't understood why I needed to talk to Elgar before I went thieving with her, but if all this about the heart stones got sorted out somehow, I might need to go back to this job.

The tail of her cloak flapped around the edge. Her hood crept into view, followed by her frowning face. She made a little shooing motion. Hurry up, it said in the most annoying way possible.

I let go of the latch and ran back to duck in next to her. The stone of the archway should have sheltered us, but wind whipped around the corner and sent my hair stinging into my eyes.

"What's taking so long?" Shan pinched the top of her hood to keep it in place. "If you have to talk to Elgar, do it. We have to get going."

"Pay me first." I stuck my hand out, palm up.

"What?"

"Pay me before I tell Elgar I'm not working until after New Year."

She dug into a pocket in the lining of her cloak, her lip curling. "You could help me because it's the right thing to do, you know."

"I'm not going out to buy cream cakes and a silk shirt." The edge of her blowing cloak wrapped around my hand. I batted it away. "My brother and I won't eat if I don't bring money home."

"How much?" Shan opened a drawstring purse.

"Two pennies a day."

She shot me a quick look.

Despite the wind, my face got hot. "Don't you think I'm worth that much? I won't cheat you. If there's a day I can work for Elgar instead of you, I'll pay you back."

"It's not that. It's— Oh, never mind." She dropped pennies into my hand and put the purse away. "Happy now?"

I counted them. When I was done, I counted again, then sorted out four coins and offered them to her. "You gave me too much."

She tucked her hands inside her cloak. "That's what I pay," she said stiffly.

I swallowed my pride and stuffed them deep into my trouser pocket.

"Go." She waved toward Elgar's.

I ran back, and this time I went in. Elgar straightened behind the counter and drummed his fingers on a list of goods. "You're late. I told you if it happened again, I'd have to dock your pay. I'm sorry, Cade, but you've made me do it."

He didn't look sorry. He looked like he'd been waiting to say that.

He consulted his list and jerked his thumb toward the door to the warehouse. "Start with a sack of flour and a small bag of sugar." When I didn't move, he lifted his head to frown at me.

Before he could speak, I drew a deep breath. "I can't work today, Elgar."

"What do you mean you can't work?"

"Not today and not until after New Year probably."

Elgar was skinny, but he was strong. Muscles bunched under his sleeve as he knotted his hand into a fist on top of the paper. "Dunnan's caught the fever now too," he said, raising his voice with each word, "so you're the only help I have. You're here, and you don't look sick. You'll work."

I shook my head. "I can't. But I'll be back after New Year."

Purple flooded up from under his beard. "I'll be hanged if you will." He pounded the counter, making the paper flutter and slide away like it was scared. "You leave me without help today, and you won't ever work for me again."

For an instant, I felt dizzy. What was I doing? I opened my mouth to say I was sorry and I'd work. "I have to go."

I lurched out the door before I could take the words back. Shan would get me into miners' houses. Besides, I didn't know if she was right about the stones stopping trouble, but she could be. After all, I knew the heart stones had power, and it had to be good for something. And I had power that had to be good for something too.

I rounded the corner and found Shan already striding away. I pelted after her. It would be all right, I told myself. Once we saved Cor City, Elgar would see why I had to do this, and he'd hire me back. Or even better, the governor would give us a big reward.

"So where are we going?" I asked.

"Master Hathen's house."

"Who's he?"

"A miner with a heart stone."

"Does he have a Finder?" I asked.

"You mean in his house?" Shan said. "I don't think so."

"We have to check," I said.

She frowned. "That'll take time, which means we're more likely to be caught."

"If you want my help, we have to look. Otherwise, I'm going back to Elgar's right now."

She must have seen I meant it, because she scowled, but nodded. "Helping Finders would be a good thing anyway. I've been thinking about what you said about what the mine is like for Finders. That's not right. Governor Barth is wrong to allow it."

I couldn't believe my luck. The first house we were going to was a miner's. If I found Mum, I wouldn't need a reward from the governor. Mum and Roth and I could all be gone by tonight.

Shan and I turned into Outer Circle Road and passed Cild's Gate, one of the old ones left standing when the wall was knocked down because they held the gods' eyes, the sacred lights that always burned. This one's flame bent sideways in the wind, and so did I, struggling to stay upright and walk at the same time.

"This weather is so bad, it's unnatural," I said.

"Of course it's unnatural." Shan gave me a startled look. "I told you. It's the start of what will happen at midnight on New Year's Eve."

Ahead, two Watchmen crouched next to an old woman who lay on her side, her gray hair spilling over the cobbles. I couldn't see her face, but her outflung arm was so thickly covered in rash that it looked burned. Pus had crusted over part of it. She didn't move when a Watchman prodded her with a cloak-wrapped finger. He backed away and grimaced at his partner. "Better send for the corpse cart."

My brain swirled. The edges of my vision turned black.

Shan caught my cloak and dragged me in a wide arc around the woman. "If we succeed, we'll stop that from happening all over the city."

I looked back. I'd seen dead people before, of course. My dad. An old man with lung fever that Mum had looked after. A neighbor woman and her baby, both dead in the birthing. But I'd never seen a body lying alone in the street.

The road curved, and I lost sight of the dead woman. I took a deep breath. Maybe I should stay in Cor and help Shan even if I did find Mum. It would only be until New Year. But no. That would risk Mum's safety, and I'd done her enough damage already.

Shan pulled me behind a statue of Corbald, the last Midland king before the syndicates took over. Pigeons huddled on the downwind side, adding to the splatter of droppings along the royal left arm. So much for eternal glory.

"That's Hathen's house." Shan nodded to the house just ahead of us.

The front gates were open to admit an important looking man and his two attendants, so I could see the house pretty well. It was two stories with glass windows and a red clay tiled roof, an ordinary rich man's house. So why was I panting like I was about to sneak into a wolf den?

"Can't you just explain how important this is and ask for the stone?" I said.

"I did ask a miner once." Shan's face hardened at the memory. "He said the temple's power was just superstition, and I was stupid to believe in it. He said he needed the stone for himself and his household. So no. We can't just ask for it. Come on." Shan hustled across the road into the walkway between Hathen's garden wall and the neighbor's. I guessed we were heading for a back gate like the one leading to the Crows' Hole, but when we got to the rear wall, it was unbroken.

"Now what?" I asked.

"Now we go over the wall." She pointed to the circles of protection carved into the wall. "Can you climb these?"

I gripped the bottom of a circle. "When we get in, we look for a Finder first."

"Depends on where we get in."

"If we're not doing that, I'm not going at all."

She rolled her eyes. "All right."

I shoved my toes into a crack in the wall. As soon as I shifted my weight, my foot slipped and slammed to the ground. I tried again and could almost see over the top when I missed a step and started to fall. Shan put her hands on my rump and shoved. I clung to the wall like a lizard.

"Make sure no one's there," she whispered and boosted me up.

I peeked over the top into a kitchen garden. Even within the walls, wind ruffled the herbs and carrot tops. The yard was empty, and the kitchen door was closed. Its windows were unshuttered, though, so anyone looking would see us. I heaved myself over and hung for a moment before dropping into a bed of rosemary whose scent exploded around me. I bounced to my feet and ran to put a jutting chimney between me and the kitchen. When Shan lowered herself over the wall, she landed more gracefully than I had, but she still smashed some mint.

She darted across the garden and tucked herself in next to me, then slid along the wall until she reached a door. The clotheslines shaking in the wind told me it probably led to the laundry. Shan tried the latch. The door opened, and she slipped inside.

I scuttled after her and fought the wind to pull the door shut, remembering at the last instant to do it softly. Dust motes danced in the light filtering through the closed shutters. As I'd guessed, stone laundry tubs ranged along one wall and an unlit boiler hunched in a corner. Shirts and underwear were heaped next to a second door, their sweaty smell mixing with the rosemary and mint we'd ground into our clothes. My stomach growled, evidently hoping one of us was a roast lamb.

Shan bent to put her mouth by my ear. "Do you feel the heart stone?"

I shook my head. "If it's small, I have to be pretty close. Where would the Finder be?"

"Working with Hathen if that man at the gates is buying a stone. Otherwise, locked in the servant quarters, which are undoubtedly on the other side of this door." She pressed her ear against the second door, then tried the latch. "Curse it." She scowled over her shoulder. "The fools keep it locked."

Fools. Right. She must think the word meant "people who get in my way."

I edged toward the yard door, thinking we'd have to try a different path in, but from her cloak, she produced a ring of slim metal tools. She crouched in front of the lock. I rose to my toes and peered over her shoulder. The lock gave a faint click, and Shan laughed quietly. She tucked the tools away.

"Where did you learn to pick locks and sneak around like this?" I asked.

For a moment, she was silent with her hand on the latch. "My governess taught me lock picking after my father took to shutting me up for weeks on end. I taught myself sneaking because when he was annoyed, it wasn't a good idea to be anywhere in his sight." She cracked open the door and slithered through.

I was pinned in place by the picture of her being frightened enough to hide from her father. Given that she'd walked out the front door of a house with the owner's heart stone, I wouldn't have thought Shan was afraid of anything.

A man's voice bellowed from the back yard. "Who's been in the herbs?"

I jumped through the door after Shan, closing it behind me.

9. TOUCHING A STONE

Can you see inside a cloud?—Myst, the shapeshifter god
We were in a hallway with closed doors on both sides. For a handful of moments, we held still, waiting to see if the man would come in from the yard.

At length, Shan bent to whisper in my ear. "No Finder here."

Disappointment stabbed me in the chest. "How do you know?"

"One of the doors would be barred on the outside."

"But she could still be with Hathen, saying a stone is genuine."

Shan looked at me sidelong. "She?"

"My mum."

Shan grimaced. "Let's see."

She tip-toed along the hallway, silent as a cat. I eased my feet down but still made more noise. No one was in sight, but male voices boomed from somewhere ahead. We passed the foot of a narrow stairway and two more closed doors. The voices grew louder.

Shan nodded toward the talking men. "That's the heartroom

ahead. The stone is probably there. Feel it?"

I shook my head impatiently. At the moment, I only cared if Mum was there.

Shan crept to the hallway's end and peeked out so I had to lean to look around her. A folding screen blocked our view. I'd seen screens like this hiding servant quarters when I worked for Elgar.

"Go in," Shan murmured.

On the other side of the screen, a man gave a braying laugh. I flinched, took a deep breath, and baby-stepped to the edge of the screen. Pulling my cloak tight around me so it wouldn't show, I tilted my head to see into the room.

Two men sat at a table with mugs in their hands. A red stone lay between them, and their heads were bent over it. I scanned the room. The men were the only people there. I pulled back next to Shan, swearing under my breath.

"I'm sorry." Shan waited a moment. "Is the stone there?"

I frowned. "Maybe." There'd been a red stone, but I felt no pull from it, and yet, it had to be here. What kind of fool kept a heart stone somewhere other than the center of the house? I crept back in and leaned around the edge of the screen again.

Nothing.

I drew back and rejoined Shan. "Are you sure Hathen has a heart stone?"

"I've seen it."

"Where?" I asked.

"His wife wears it in a necklace sometimes."

"Well, the only stone in there is fake."

Shan stiffened. "There'd better be a real one somewhere, or we're in trouble." She started back down the hallway. "We'll have to search the house." She ignored the closed rooms on either side of us, which made sense since something as precious as a heart stone was unlikely to be in the servant quarters. At the stairs, she peeked to make sure they were empty, then started up.

I was on the second step, watching Shan vanish around a landing, when I caught my toe and sprawled forward. My hands jammed into a riser, and one knee rammed a stair. I muffled my howl, but someone had left a pair of silver cups on the bottom step, and they clattered on the hallway floor like a herd of dancing ponies.

Shan darted back into sight above me, beckoning urgently as a door opened in the hall. I ran up the stairs and ducked around the corner with her.

"I know it was you," a woman called from below.

Oh gods, she must have seen me.

"The cups are there to be carried up by the next one going, Wynath," the woman called. "You want me to tell the mistress how lazy you are?"

Heavy footsteps thudded on the stairs.

I scrambled after Shan. In the wide hallway stretching toward the front of the house, she put her ear to the first door, yanked it open, and dove in with me stepping on her skirt, tripping both of us. I kicked over a broom propped against the wall, but Shan caught it before it hit anything. I pulled the door almost shut but left a crack to spy through.

I squeezed against Shan's side, while she squeezed against the other wall. We were in a closet full of brooms and buckets. It was a gods' gift I hadn't knocked the whole bunch out into the hall. I shifted away from a knob digging into my right shoulder, attached to what looked like a cupboard that was probably full of more noisy things for me to toss around.

A maid came out of the servants' stairwell and strode past carrying the two mugs. She opened a door across the hall, took a step into the room, and froze.

"Oh good, you've brought cups," an unseen woman said coolly. "I was about to send for them. They should have been here to start with. My guest and I have had to wait."

The maid bobbed a curtsy. "Sorry, Mistress. Shall I pour the wine?" She went into the room, wiping the cups on the side of her apron farthest from the unseen woman.

The door swung shut behind her. I started to ease the closet door open, but Shan reached over my shoulder to stop its movement.

"Wait," she murmured, her breath tickling my ear.

A moment later, the maid came back into the hallway. She looked both ways, frowning, and closed the door. "Wynath?" she called softly. "Are you trying to get me into trouble?" Her scowl deepened, and she was muttering to herself when she passed the closet and disappeared down the stairs.

I glanced at Shan. When she nodded, we slipped into the hallway. Shan crept past the room where Hathen's wife was entertaining her guest. I shifted from foot to foot as Shan listened at the next door, then opened it and went in. A huge bed filled the center of the room. Clothes chests, a washstand, and a dressing table crowded along every inch of wall space except for a door that undoubtedly connected this room with the one where Hathen's wife sat. The moment I stepped over the doorsill, a tingle ran up my spine.

I turned slowly, then stopped, facing a chest on the far wall. My feet moved there on their own, and I lifted the lid. Something made of yellow silk glimmered on top of the pile of folded clothes, but on one side, a box was built in. I touched its smooth wood, then tried to open it. Locked.

Shan came up next to me. "There?" She got out her ring of tools and set to work. The box clicked, and she opened it.

It was divided into three velvet-lined sections, one holding a string of pearls, one a jade bracelet, and the third a gleaming, red heart stone caught in a cage of thin gold threads and suspended from a gold chain. It was tear shaped and about the size of a walnut.

Before I could stop myself, I picked it up. My knee had been hurting from when I'd whacked it on the stairs. Now the pain faded. A throb like a drum beat pulsed in my belly. Warmth flowed through me, and the muscles in my back relaxed.

Shan grabbed the necklace, my fingers closing too late to keep her from scooping it out of my hand. "You shouldn't touch it," she said.

"I know." Shocked by how hard I wanted to take the stone back, I twisted my fists in my cloak.

Shan fumbled inside her cloak again, and brought out a red stone identical to the one in the necklace. With one of her tools, she prodded at the gold cage around the heart stone. In a moment, she had the stone free and was replacing it with the one she'd brought.

"How did you know what it looked like?" I whispered, never taking my eyes off the stone.

"Sometimes we have to make two trips, the first to see what we should make the fake stone look like and the second to make the switch." She drew a gold thread into place. "But I've seen her wear this necklace more than once." She tucked the heart stone and her tools into her cloak. Then she put the necklace back in the jewelry box and closed both it and the chest.

The voice of Hathen's wife came from the next room. "The silk is a wonderful color. I'll show it to you." Her voice was growing louder.

I jumped for the hallway door, where Shan was already listening. The latch on the connecting door rattled.

"No trouble at all," Hathen's wife said.

Shan yanked the door open, and we scrambled through. I glimpsed the connecting door opening through the last crack of space before Shan silently closed our door. We ran toward the stairway, only to hear someone coming up.

"Well, if it wasn't you, Wynath, then who was it?" The maid sounded indignant.

I looked around wildly. Shan grabbed my arm and dragged me back into the broom closet. It wouldn't be good enough. It they thought someone was in the house, they'd surely search in there. Panic washed through my gut. I had no idea how Governor Barth would punish Shan, but he'd send me to the mine.

Shan yanked open the cupboard door. "Climb in."

I stared at her, open-mouthed.

"Do it!" she said.

I pulled myself up and found it wasn't a cupboard after all, but a wooden chute of some sort. I swung my feet into the opening, lowered myself until my arms were straight, and let go.

I plunged down, bouncing from side to side with teeth-clacking impacts. Before I had time to picture anything beyond fire or upward-pointing spikes, I landed in a pile of cloth. The stink of stale sweat puffed up around me. Across from me was a row of stone sinks. I was in the laundry room.

A whoosh came from overhead, and I rolled out of the way as Shan fell out of the chute. She stumbled to her feet, settling her skirt around her legs.

I opened the yard door a crack. No one there. We rushed out into the yard. The wind tangled my cloak around my legs. As I tugged it free, I spotted a trellis against the stone wall. I touched Shan's arm. The instant she saw what I was looking at, she ran toward it, waving for me to climb it first.

I scaled the trellis, yanking my cloak and trousers free of thorns as I went. The trellis creaked way too much like the window in the shack behind the jeweler's had, but I was at the top of the wall now. I let myself down into a passageway between Hathen's house and the neighbor's back garden, then waited for Shan to appear.

A moment later, Shan dropped, almost on top of me, and bolted at once. I followed her into a maze of passageways until we came out onto a dirt lane with a pump at the corner. Gasping for air, we crouched on the downwind side of the pump, me trying to ignore the pull of the stone she had hidden in her cloak.

When her breathing had eased, Shan dropped her head back against the stone base of the pump and laughed. "Good work, Cade. Thank the gods you came after me the other day. I thought every Finder in the city was under such close guard I'd never get near them."

I'd just put my finger through a little hole the thorns had ripped in my thigh and, even worse, in my only pair of trousers. I'd heal on my own, but the trousers wouldn't. Still, I was elated. I hadn't found Mum yet, but helping Shan gave me a way to look in miners' houses. Besides I liked being around the stone even if I couldn't touch it. "How would you know where every Finder was? We don't exactly brag about what we can do."

"True. I was reduced to checking the list and guessing which Finders might have Finder relatives."

I frowned. "What list?"

"The one the miners' syndicate keeps of their assets, where they're using them, where they found them."

"Assets?" I said. "You mean people. Where is this list?"

She shifted, then straightened to her feet. "Syndicate House. The current governor is head of the miners' syndicate, so their office is there." She looked both ways along the street.

"You saw this list?" I stood up next to her.

"A friend who works there looked at it for me. She's also the one I asked about when Jem would be tried."

I opened my mouth to ask more, but she spoke first.

"I have to take this heart stone to a safe place, and then I have to be somewhere. We should meet at that same archway—same time—tomorrow, but in the meantime, I have a job for you."

She'd paid me for all day, so I shut up and listened.

"Hathen's house was the last one I was certain had a heart stone," she said.

"Governor Barth has one. A big one. I felt it even through his garden wall."

She watched a beat-up straw hat cartwheel along the street, driven by the wind. "Syndicate House is too well guarded. So I want you to scout near all the other big houses and see if you can sense more stones. New Year is only four days away, and we still need two stones. If I have to make two trips to get each, that's not a lot of time."

"All right." We started walking. "Shan, what you said about your father. Does he still..." I trailed off, not knowing what to say. When Dad died, I felt like the world had ended, like a big hole had opened up and Mum and Roth and me were all teetering on the edge. I still missed him so bad it hurt sometimes. I couldn't imagine what it would be like to feel like Shan did.

"I don't really care any more." She hugged her cloak tight around her. "He'd not want me doing this, and you'll notice I am anyway." She flashed me a smile. "I find that makes it even more fun."

"Does your mum—"

"She died when I was born."

"Sorry," I said.

Her mouth twisted. "I didn't know her, so you wouldn't think I could miss her, but I do. I gather you live with your brother?"

I nodded.

Wind whipped our cloaks out behind us like wings. We walked together to the Inner Circle, where she pointed me in one direction, before she and the heart stone went off in the other.

I struggled along, fighting the wind, and pausing at every house's gate. I lingered longest at the ones with the miners' pickaxe symbol carved on the gate post. I meant to search those even if I had to lie to Shan about feeling a stone there. I stopped at another gate and stood on tiptoe to see through the bars. A stone would have to be as big as Governor Barth's for me to sense it from the road, but it had happened before when gates and windows and doors stood open.

It was odd to be roaming around during the day. When we first started looking for Mum, Roth said we had to work at the same place. It wasn't until the foreman hit me hard enough to knock me down that Roth let me work apart from him with Elgar, who was cheap but decent.

I'd felt free enough without Roth breathing down my neck all day. Wandering along on my own like this, I felt like I'd been tied up but had now broken loose.

I'd walked about halfway around the circle when a young man reeled sideways and stumbled into me. I grabbed his arm to steady him and me both. He peered at me through dull eyes. Spots of red flamed on his cheeks, but the rest of his face was gray and beaded with sour-smelling sweat.

Fever.

I let go and took a step back, but he swayed, and if I hadn't caught him, he'd have fallen. He was maybe Roth's age, so he should have been much too strong to fall sick. I remembered the Watchman wrapping his finger in his cloak before he touched the dead woman and hastily shifted my hand to put the sick man's sleeve between his skin and mine. I couldn't leave him in the street. I'd just take him somewhere as fast as I could.

"Where do you live?" I asked.

"Don't want to go home." He pointed to a passage between two big houses. "There. My friend got better in there."

I guided him down the passage. Could one of these houses have a heart stone?

"By the gate," he said.

On the left, a barred gate pierced the wall. I eased him down to lean against it and looked through the bars at the house. The shutters and doors were closed on this side of the house, but was that a wisp of power I felt? I closed my eyes and made myself relax. A shiver slipped over my skin. Yes! This house had a heart stone. And a good thing too because on top of the odd weather, seeing this sick young man and the dead old woman had finally convinced me Shan was right. Trouble was coming. If heart stones didn't cure it, I didn't know what we'd do.

I eyed the sick man slumped against the gate. "You all right? You want me to get anyone?"

He shook his head and waved me away. "This is good. This will help."

I hoped so. I went back to the road and started searching again. If the fever was spreading, there was no time to waste.

10. THE LIST

Great strength means great struggle.—Sceld, the hero god

I'd found one of the two stones we needed, but the afternoon was only half gone. I didn't want to cheat Shan, and New Year was only four days away, New Year's Eve only three. So I kept searching.

The road circled around to Syndicate House. Judging from the row of carriages parked at the roadside, Governor Barth was having a party. I thought about the list of mining company "assets" that Shan had mentioned, the list of Finders. I wanted to know if it said where Mum was. With a party going on, there'd be lots of strangers going in and out of Syndicate House. They'd never notice one more.

The drivers had gathered out of the wind between the row of carriages and the garden wall. I trailed my hand along the wall as I walked toward them. The power of Governor Barth's heart stone throbbed against my fingertips.

"She can't get out of bed, she's that sick," a driver with a curly beard said. He held gloves in one hand and kept tapping them against his trouser seam.

"It's just summer fever." A gray-haired driver flicked his hand, fluffing away the other man's worry. "Lots of people have it."

"And they're sicker than I've ever seen," a third man said. A sharp line creased the space between his eyebrows. "A little tyke in my road died last night. I'm beginning to think folks are right when they say something will happen when the calendar changes. Makes me wish I had one of those stones."

Curly-beard's worried gaze caught on me. "Did you want something, lad?"

"I've a message for the miners' syndicate. Will anyone be in the office with this going on?" I jerked my thumb toward the carriages.

"It's a syndicate party," Curly-beard said. "They won't want business stopped. The clerk will be there. Tell the gate guard, and he'll take you in."

I looked toward the gate. Last chance to decide this was a stupid thing to do.

Gray-hair nudged my shoulder. "Go on."

I walked to the gate, brain busy spinning my tale. My heart beat so hard that my whole body vibrated.

The gate Crow looked straight ahead, his black tabard rippling in the wind.

"Excuse me," I said, and he frowned down at me. "I'm supposed to take a message to the syndicate office."

"Give it to me, and I'll see it gets there." He put out a hand.

"It's not written down."

He called through the doorway of box-sized building. "Wilder, take the boy to the office."

A second Crow emerged, pulling on his helmet. He must be Wilder. Unfortunately, he also was the Crow who'd chased me off from the

Crows' Hole the day before.

I looked down, making my hands stay where they were no matter how much they wanted to come up and cover my face. He'd just glimpsed me the once, and he'd been miserable with rain. He couldn't possibly recognize me.

He crooked his finger, and I followed a pace behind as he strode toward the house front door. "Do you need to see someone in particular?" he asked.

"Just the clerk," I mumbled to the cobblestones.

A loud crack sounded, and I jumped and looked up to find the wind snapping the pennants outside the front door. I bumped into something solid and nearly fell, but a vise closed on my arm.

Wilder had stopped and was looking down at my upturned face. It was his hand on my arm. "You're the one who came to the jail yesterday." He narrowed his eyes. "Message, eh? Maybe you should tell it to my captain."

"It's confidential." The words tripped over one another trying to get out of my mouth. "I'm supposed to tell it to the clerk." My heart knocked against my ribs so hard, I was surprised Wilder didn't hear it.

"Right." Wilder wrenched my arm up behind my back and dragged me into Syndicate House.

From the heartroom at the far end of the hall came music and the sound of people talking and laughing. A girl in a bright yellow dress danced past the doorway in the arms of an older man. The smells of sweat and hot cinnamon drifted down the hall.

Wilder hauled me into a room just inside the front door. A Crow wearing a captain's blue sash looked up from the papers on his desk. He had sharp eyes the same color as the sash. I looked at the floor.

"Captain Menard, sir, it's the boy I told you about," Wilder said. "The one who tried to bring something to the thieving Finder."

"His mum sent me," I said. "I didn't know he was a thief. I hate thieves. But he's not why I'm here today. I have a message for the syndicate clerk. That's—"

"Shut up." Captain Menard spoke casually, a man used to being obeyed.

I clamped my mouth closed, crunching up the words still swirling around in there.

Menard leaned back in his chair and scratched his beard. "The thief's neighbor, are you?"

I was still swallowing words, so I just nodded.

He cocked his head. "I wonder if that's true. Is it possible you're a thief and a Finder too? Someone the prisoner worked with? We know he had an accomplice."

"No." I shook my head. "No, no, no. I have a message for the clerk, but if you don't want to let me in, I'll just go." I tried to pull away from Wilder and show this officer how willing I was to get out of his sight.

He snorted, then nodded at Wilder. The Crow let me go. I turned to see him leave the room and started after him, but he shut the door in my face.

"Sit." Menard came around his desk, put a hand on my shoulder, and pressed me onto a stool. He sat on the desk, looming over me and smiling unpleasantly. Sweat gathered in my armpits. We waited, though I had no idea for what.

The door opened. Menard put one hand on my head so I couldn't turn to see who it was, and the other on the side of my neck. He pressed two fingers against my pulsing vein. Nobody said anything.

Menard took his hand away and looked over my head. "No reaction, so not a Finder anyway."

I blinked. What test had he just done to get such a wrong answer? I swiveled on the stool. Wilder stood there, holding an open, jewel-trimmed box. Nestled in the velvet lining was a small red stone. I'd felt the presence of a heart stone even from the street, but wherever it was in this house, it wasn't in the box Wilder held. That stone was a fake. Shan must already have done her light-fingered work here.

I faked a cough and hid my smile behind my hand.

Menard grabbed my collar and drew me to my feet, choking off any desire I felt to smile. His unblinking gaze bored into me like a tunneling mole. "Do you really have a message for the clerk?" He twisted his hand, and my collar tightened. "Because if you do, I'll take you to see him myself."

I should probably say no and get out of there. "I really do have a message."

"All right, then." He let go of my shirt, and I shrugged it back into place. A scowling Wilder opened the door for us, and Menard steered me out into the hallway where music from the heartroom washed over us before he knocked on another door and shoved me inside. Like Captain Menard, the clerk sat behind a desk, but the clerk was skinny and round shouldered. He scowled like the captain, though, and sounded much crabbier.

"What is it?" the clerk asked.

"The boy says he has a message for you." Menard stood where he could see my face.

"Let's hear it," the clerk said. "I'm busy."

I swallowed what little spit there was in my mouth. "Olstaff the jeweler sent me. He thinks he saw a woman who was rented to him as an appraiser but who ran away. He wants to know if the miners have any record of her. Maybe they picked her up by accident and know where she is now?"

I held my breath. Menard watched me like a cat with both eyes on a mouse hole.

The clerk reached for a ledger on a shelf behind him and opened it on his desk. "Name?"

"Mareth, Aruld's widow." Her name made a warm spot in the chilly room.

The clerk flipped pages until he came to the one he wanted, then ran an ink-stained finger along the list of names. I tried to read them upside down but couldn't. His finger stopped moving. "She was picked up a little more than two weeks ago and sent to work in the Malel family's mine." He looked up frowning. "Are you sure you have the right name? They took her to the mine."

"Maybe this Malel brought her back to Cor City and rented her to someone," I said, though "rented her to someone" was hard to spit out. "Can you tell if that happened?"

"Malel should have reported it if he did," the clerk said, "but sometimes miners think a secret Finder gives them an advantage in hunting out fake stones. Though in that case, Malel wouldn't have rented her out."

"You mean an advantage in selling fake stones." My voice shook. "A miner wouldn't want to give up an advantage that lets him do that. They always need more."

Captain Menard straightened and narrowed his eyes. "Would you care to repeat that?"

An alarm drum beat in the back of my head. "No."

"Smart boy. The miners' syndicate is just following the law. You might not like a law, but if you believe in order, you should show some respect." Menard waved toward the door. "Out."

He followed me into the hallway, where Wilder waited, though he'd stowed the box somewhere. "This was another of your Finder vendettas, Wilder," Menard said. "Keep your mind on your job, or you won't have one. Show him out."

Red-faced, Wilder seized my arm and dragged me out of the house. In the courtyard, he stopped and bent to speak in my ear, his hot breath sliding under my collar. "You think you're smart, don't you? Well, you can fool that prissy captain, but you can't fool me. I know what you are. Your sort turns my stomach. If I so much as see you blink within a mile of a heart stone, I'll arrest you and take you straight to Governor Barth. He's a miner. He knows how well Finders lie."

He planted a hand between my shoulder blades and shoved me across to the gate, where the Crow I'd first spoken to waited. Wilder gripped the top of my head and turned my face toward him.

"If this one shows up again, put him in a cell. Then come get me," Wilder said.

He let go of me, and I scurried to get out the gate, so it didn't hurt much when he drove the heel of his boot into my backside.

I hustled across the road and into a narrow alley. Gradually, my heart and I both slowed. Tomorrow, I'd ask Shan which house belonged to Malel because that's where Mum would be. I'd free her, and then she, Roth, and I would be on our way to safety.

11. ANOTHER THIEF

A puddle in every path.—Ras, the trickster god

It was late enough for me to buy supper and go home, so I headed for the market. I felt a little guilty about lying to Roth, so I went to the stall selling the mustard sausage that was his favorite, even though it did cost more.

I bounced on my toes while the merchant waited on a woman buying enough to feed a pack of wild dogs. How big was her household anyway? I kept an eye on the tray of mustard sausage, hoping there'd be some left.

"You having company for New Year, Mistress?" The sausage seller added another packet to what she'd already bought.

"Not likely. We're gathering supplies and leaving town until it's over." She brushed her wind-whipped hair back from her face.

"If you believe in the old prophecies of doom, how's leaving Cor City going to help?" the dealer asked. "I heard the bridge collapsed over Three Mile Gorge, and Saddler's Town has set a guard to keep out folks carrying fever."

"Half the people on my street are sick," she said, "and this weather can't be natural. They say whatever happens will be worst here at the world's center, so we're taking no chances." She tossed all her purchases into a basket and hurried away.

I watched her go. If only she knew that Shan and I were going to save her and everyone else too.

"You think that's funny?" The sausage seller's face was pinched with worry.

I wiped away my smile. "Of course not." I bought the sausage and left. When I looked back, the merchant was staring toward where the woman had gone.

I beat Roth home but not by much. I was just putting the plates on the table when he strode in, slamming the door behind him. Without speaking, he plunked the jug of cider on the table and went straight out to the privy we shared with nine other families. The wind caught the back door, and he had to struggle to close it.

"Curse this city and everyone in it." He slammed that door too. When he came back in, he stomped to the table, sat down, and rubbed his hands over his face. The wind whistled down our lane, flinging dirt at the half-open shutters.

"What's the matter?" I asked.

"Nothing. Just work."

"I bought mustard sausage." I shoved it a little closer to him. "I got paid extra today."

He let his hands fall away and looked at the sausage. When he lifted his gaze to me, he smiled. "Maybe not everyone should be cursed."

"What are brothers for?" I grinned.

"This is just for today, though. We should be saving any extra money. We'll need every penny for getting away." He reached for the knife to divide our food.

What did I expect? He was still Roth.

"Where did you and Elgar go today?" Roth asked.

"Nowhere interesting." I stuffed bread in my mouth to keep guilty words from jumping out.

#

When I tried to leave the next morning, Roth still sat at the table, scratching his stomach and looking even more worn down than usual.

"Wait." With perfect bad timing, he hauled himself upright and came out with me. I swear he could smell I had a secret. "I'm coming with you," he said.

"You're walking me to work? How old do you think I am?"

"Old enough to get into real trouble."

"In the day?"

"The Watch hasn't found the heart stone thief yet, so they'll be looking for Finders. If we didn't need the money, I'd make you stay home."

"You could try," I said.

He swatted the back of my head. "Better you should have Elgar keeping an eye on you anyway."

A faint rumbling sounded in the distance.

"Was that thunder?" Roth said. "It sounded odd."

"It's just far away. Where are you working today?" Maybe I'd get lucky, and he'd have to go in a different direction before we got to the arch where I was meeting Shan.

"Same place as yesterday. We didn't get as much work as we should have done on account of the wind, and the foreman said he'd fire anyone who was late today." Roth's voice was tight. Yesterday must have been bad for him. I wished with everything in me that he could be working in a lawyer's office.

"Cade," a woman called. "Cade, wait."

Tricky gods. Shan.

I turned, and so did Roth. Shan hurried toward us, a wide smile softening her thin face. She wore her maid's apron, carried a marketing basket, and looked cheery as a buttercup.

"It's lucky I saw you," she said. "It saves us both some walking."

Roth's eyes slid toward Shan and back to me.

"I'll see you tonight, Roth." I tried to walk away, but Roth caught my arm.

"Introduce us, Cade," he said.

"Shan, this is my brother, Roth. Roth, this is Shan. She's—" I groped for an explanation Roth would swallow. "Elgar loaned me to work for her for a few days."

"What kind of work?" Roth sounded pleasant, but he kept hold of my arm.

"He's helping me shop for my master's New Year party." Shan put her basket in my free hand and smiled at Roth. "Cade carries the packages for me."

"He didn't mention that. Would you excuse us a moment?" Roth pulled me a few yards down the lane and spoke quietly. "She's the source of the extra money to buy the mustard sausage? What are you really doing?"

"I'm carrying packages." I held up Shan's basket. "Is something wrong with that?"

"You tell me. Elgar's business isn't providing under-servants. And why is her master paying for one when he undoubtedly has other servants already? Why does she have money to hand out?" He glanced at Shan, who wiggled her fingers in a little wave. One corner of his mouth quirked like he was fighting a smile. "She's pretty. That's not making you do something stupid, is it?"

I frowned at Shan. "So far, you're the only one of us who's been stupid over a girl," I said.

Scowling now, he dragged his gaze back to me. "What are you talking about?"

"That one with the long braid? She batted her eyelashes, and you fell all over yourself. I heard you practicing what you were going to say to her, and even I knew it was hopeless. She was probably glad when we left. And the niece of that butcher in Yellow Dog Lane? She—"

"None of that is your business." Roth's face was red. "And it's not what we're talking about now. Who is this Shan? I don't like you going around with someone I don't know."

"Elgar loaned me to her," I repeated.

Roth drew a deep breath and slowly loosened his grip on me. "I guess I trust Elgar." His mouth twisted. "Still, if you get into trouble, you better hope the Watch catches you before I do." He nodded to Shan and set off for work.

Shan came up beside me, looking toward where Roth had turned out of sight. "I was afraid he might try to stop you helping me."

"He wanted to. He thinks he's in charge of the world."

"He's protective. That's not a bad thing. Some men would let their families drown if it furthered their own ambition."

I thought again about why she said she'd learned to sneak. Maybe "protective" sounded good when your father scared you. I could tell her it sounded a whole lot less appealing when your brother thought you needed his help to blow your nose.

"Did you find more stones?" Shan asked.

"I found a house that for sure has one, and I heard some people saying a friend of theirs was cured of fever outside another one—the Malels'. Do you know where they live?" I held my breath.

"The Malels?" Shan asked. "They have an estate in the country and almost never come to town. When they do, they rent a place, so I'm not sure where they are. I'll ask around."

Excitement fizzed in my chest like strong ale. Soon I'd know where Mum was.

"So where's the house with the stone?" Shan asked.

I guided her down a lane toward the richer part of town, both of us skipping out of the path of a donkey cart piled with last harvest's shriveled carrots and potatoes. As it had earlier, a thunder-like noise groaned from somewhere, strong enough that the ground shimmied. The donkey squealed in terror and bolted, the driver cursing and dragging on the reins. I had to brace my hand on the rough wooden wall of a chandler's shop so I wouldn't fall.

"That's the energy shift," Shan said. "It'll get worse and worse until we put the stones in the temple."

Maybe I should look for another house with a stone rather than steering Shan to the Malels'. "What if we don't?"

"You saw the murals," she said grimly.

The Malels probably really did have a heart stone, I reassured myself. They were miners after all, and with fever going around, they'd surely keep a heart stone in the house.

We followed the Inner Circle until I spotted the house where I'd left the sick young man. We stopped while Shan ran her gaze over walls, windows, roof, everything. If she looked at my house like that, I'd expect to come home to find even the cobwebs missing. I frowned. A guard loomed at the front gate, and another lurked in the entrance to the side passage where I'd taken the sick man.

"Those guards weren't here yesterday," I said. "I bet they've heard someone's taking heart stones."

From behind, power trembled over me. Another ground shaker? No, wait. The buzz rippling over my skin meant only one thing. Two men passed us, going toward the front gate. One wore a fine linen shirt and carried a leather bag with the miners' pickaxe crest.

"He's carrying at least one heart stone," I whispered to Shan. I started after him, but Shan grabbed me and nodded toward the second man, who carried a big club covered in spikes.

"Don't be a fool," Shan said.

"But we need two more stones, and the house is guarded." I struggled in her grip. "You distract the guard, and I'll grab that bag before they go in."

"No," she said. "That club would smash your skull like a melon."

"Your voice is too high, or I'd swear you were Roth."

The house gate opened, and the men went inside. The gate closed behind them, locking away the heart stone.

"You see?" I said. "Now what?"

"Let's try the back." Shan hurried to the end of the block and around to the narrow alley running behind the houses. The alley reeked of fish guts. I trotted after her. She hastened only a few yards into the alley before jamming to a halt. Another guard paced along the house's back wall. He shot us a sharp look, and we backed out into the side street so fast my shoes skidded in fish slop.

"Any other ideas?" I asked.

"Let me think." Shan led me back to the Inner Circle, where she scanned the house and chewed her lower lip, while I rocked from fishy foot to fishy foot, worrying.

The front gate opened again, and the guard came out. My breath quickened. I plucked at Shan's sleeve and nodded after the guard.

"What?" She was still studying the house.

"The guard has a heart stone," I said.

She whipped around to look at the guard's departing back. "He shouldn't."

We looked at one another.

"He's a thief," I said gleefully. "Whatever we do, he won't be able to complain. Come on."

We hustled after the thieving guard. The fancy Inner Circle wasn't a good place to try to wrestle the stone away from him, but fortunately he soon turned off and began to weave his way through the dirt lanes and side alleys. We were drawing closer when he ducked into the Tall Tankard Tavern. The tavern's shutters were closed, despite it being day, probably because both hinges on the left one were broken. White paint peeled off the shutters and the door in flakes like a disgusting disease.

We lingered in the shadow of a stable. On the other side of the wall, horses were stomping and snorting. The sound and smell of them were comforting, reminding me of when I worked for Master Joff and went home to a family at night.

"How are we going to do this?" Shan said. "I'm better at sneaking than street brawls."

"We might not have to brawl," I said. "If he stays in that tavern long enough, he'll be a lot less alert when he comes out." But just then, the Tall Tankard's door opened, and the guard came out and strolled away, whistling "The Mummer's Girl" and swinging his club.

Shan took a step after him, but I stopped her. "He doesn't have the stone any more," I said.

We both looked at the Tall Tankard.

"Let's go in," Shan said.

I hadn't been in many taverns, because Mum finally threatened to take a switch to me, though all I was doing was seeing what they were like. But I'd been in enough to know the kind of man who'd be in this dump.

"You'd stick out like a skunk at a squirrel social. I'll go," I said. She was still sputtering as I strode across the road into the Tall Tankard.

My skin itched, so there was a heart stone in there all right. The question was where. I stood just inside the dark, smoky room, waiting for my eyes to adjust. The place smelled like ten years of spilled ale. Two men sat at separate tables, though the tavern keeper was nowhere in sight. I hoped he wasn't off stowing a heart stone in the cellar.

I drifted toward the closest drinker, hunched over his mug like a new mum over her baby. He cut his red-rimmed eyes sideways at me as I passed. The itching grew stronger. The second man raised a head of greasy hair to blink at me. He wore a filthy neck cloth and equally revolting cap and looked as likely to have a heart stone as he did a pet bear, but he had one anyway.

I edged toward the tavern door. This was the kind of guy you didn't want to turn your back on. A hand grabbed my wrist. My heart jumped up into my throat, which was the only reason I didn't shriek. But it was the first man, the one who looked like ale was his only reason to live.

"You. Boy." He shoved an empty mug toward me, leaving a trail of spilled ale. A roach scurried through it and disappeared over the table edge. "Get me another."

"I don't work here." I tried to pull free, but his fingers tightened.

With his other hand, he thumped the mug on the table. "Another!"

The man with the stone watched us with narrowed eyes.

I grabbed the mug and went behind the counter. I'd seen tavern keepers fill mugs. It didn't look hard. I fumbled at the handle on the barrel. Which way did it go?

"Here!" a new voice cried.

I whirled to see a fat man in a stained apron coming through a back door. The tavern keeper!

The mug clattered to the floor as I vaulted over the counter and raced across the room.

"I should call the Watch!" the tavern keeper shouted as the door banged shut behind me.

In the bright sunlight, I had trouble seeing Shan in the shadows by the stable.

"What was that about?" Shan asked when I hustled up beside her.

"Nothing. A man in a cap has the stone," I said.

Before the last word was out of my mouth, the Tall Tankard's door opened again, and the man who had the heart stone came out. We pressed against the stable wall. He glanced both ways, blinking, then set off, going away from us.

Curse the man. He hadn't left us time to plan. At least, he didn't have a big, brain-crushing club. I led Shan after him, thinking frantically. When he turned into an alley between the two back walls, I snatched at the only idea I had.

On silent feet, I ran up closer. "Halt in the name of the Watch!" I cried in the most manly voice I could dig up. His head started to turn. "Don't turn around," I added hastily.

He froze. "What's the matter?" His tone said he was all astonished that the Watch could come after a law-abiding citizen like him.

"Drop the stone," I said.

"What stone?" he asked.

"You don't want to make my partner angry," I said.

Shan made a kind of growling noise and thwacked her basket against a wall.

"We know you have a heart stone," I said. "We were following the guard you bought it from. Now throw it back here."

"Bought it?" he whined. "I didn't buy it. I found it." He fished a heart stone from his pocket and flung it to the ground. It lay there winking at me, shaped like a pink half-moon.

I wanted it. Instead, I waved for Shan to pick it up. She scooped it off the dirt and tucked it into her apron.

"I was on my way to turn it in." Free of his guilty burden, the man swiveled toward us. He had to look down to see me. His gaze went from me to Shan, and his mouth fell open. "Here!" he cried. "Give me back that stone."

He rushed at me, sticking his hand inside his shirt and pulling out something that flashed in the sunlight. I raised both hands to ward him off. The flashing thing flicked across my side, leaving a trail of ice. I looked down and saw a knife and blood welling around the edges of a cut in my shirt. The icy trail turned to fiery pain.

He shoved me against the wall and put the knife point to my throat. "Give it back," he said. The smell of ale blew up my nostrils. My mouth went dry, which was good because I didn't dare swallow with the very sharp knife where it was.

Something flew in a blur over his head and caught around his neck—the woven straw handle of Shan's marketing basket. "Get off him!" She hauled on the basket, yanking his head back. "Leave him alone!"

His face went purple. The knife clattered to the ground as his fingers shot to scrabble at the handle biting deep into his neck. He fell backward, crushing the basket noisily between his body and the alley.

I got a quick glimpse of Shan's pale face before she said, "Come on," and ran for the other end of the alley.

I clapped my hand over my bleeding side and stumbled after her. "You have the stone?" I gasped.

"Yes." She looked back, then came to raise my hand to her shoulder and wrap her arm around me. She helped me into a side street where she spotted a gate left ajar and dragged me through. She lowered me to sit on the edge of a broken-wheeled cart.

"Turns out you can brawl after all," I wheezed. "I'm impressed."

She latched the gate, then bent to look at my side.

I looked, felt dizzy, and looked away, gulping air. My blood seeped like juice from an underdone cherry pie, and my side hurt enough that I had to grit my teeth to keep from saying so. Plus my shirt was cut and covered in gore. I had a second shirt, which was a good thing because I'd have to stuff this one under the back step until New Year was over and I could dig it out to see what I could salvage.

"Do you think he's dead?" Shan's voice trembled.

"The guy from the tavern? No, he was rolling around, cussing. Didn't you hear?"

Shan let out a long breath. "My heart was beating too loudly for me to hear anything else."

"You didn't look scared," I said. "And you did the right thing. He was slicing me like a roast chicken."

"I know. I've just never done that before." She straightened. "We have to get you to a healer."

"I can't."

"I'll pay." She took my arm and drew me to my feet, but I staggered away from her.

"It's not just the money," I said. "A healer will use a heart stone, and he'll know I'm a Finder from the way I react."

She looked at the cut again. "All right. We'll go somewhere else." She grabbed my arm more firmly, checked to see no one was in the street, and guided me out of the yard.

12. IN NEED OF HEALING

Music takes all the notes.—Mins, the musician god

I leaned on Shan, taking shallow breaths. Every step shot fire along my ribs. Shan walked on my bleeding side so no one we passed would see it, but she needn't have worried. Everyone took wide detours around us, probably thinking I was feeble with fever. We kept to alleys and lanes until Shan guided us onto the Inner Circle, close enough to Syndicate House that I could see the roof. Groggy as I was, I knew better than to walk past Governor Barth's front gate and risk Wilder being on guard duty.

I was about to say that when Shan bundled me into an alcove in a garden wall. She propped me against the wall and crouched to lift a wooden grate from a storm drain.

I'd seen those drains, of course, though only along the cobbled roads. Rain ran off into them and kept rich people's streets from flooding while we who-cares-about-them people on dirt lanes slogged through the puddles and mud.

"Get in there," Shan said.

I pushed myself shakily off the wall. "Into the sewer?"

"Get in. Quickly, before someone comes." She grabbed me under the armpits and pulled.

I muffled a grunt of pain. "Let go. I'll do it." I dropped to my knees, wriggled backward into the drain, and lowered myself. When I let go, cold water closed over my ankles. I was in a dark stone tunnel. Moss slimed the walls, and the place reeked of mold. For once, it was good to be short because I could stand straight while Shan had to hunch over when she splashed down beside me. With one hand, she held her skirt out of the water, while she reached the other through the opening and pulled the wooden grate back into place.

"This way." She put an arm around me again, and we sloshed off, keeping to the edge where the water was shallowest. A dead rat floated past. The only light came through widely spaced grates, so it was hard to see anything. When I put my free hand on the wall, my fingers squelched through some sort of muck, and I snatched them away.

"Where are we going?" I belatedly asked.

"To my old governess. She'll know how to tend that cut," Shan said.

"She lives in the sewer?"

Shan gave a short laugh. "No. She only works here." She helped me around a corner. This new stretch was dark as a moonless night, but we hadn't gone twenty yards before my pulse quickened, and my whole body hummed

Shan was carrying the heart stone we'd just taken, and I'd felt its presence all along, but now the vibration of energy got stronger. "There's a heart stone," I said.

"More than one," Shan said. "This is where we keep the stones I gather."

Dim light slanted into the tunnel ahead. When we got there, Shan squeezed us through a crack in the tunnel wall into what looked like a flooded cellar. Collapsed shelves lined the walls, and the place stank of rotting wood. The light came from a doorway at the top of some steps on the room's other side.

I wasn't feeling too hot anyway, and now my body started jangling oddly. Unless you counted the mine, I'd never been near more than one heart stone at a time. Maybe the powers of a bunch of heart stones were bumping up against one another.

Shan helped me across the room. We'd started up the short flight of stairs, when my right foot shot out from under me, and I slid out of her grip into the water. I came up sputtering and clutching my stinging side.

"Shan, who's this?" a woman said. "What's going on?"

I looked up to see an older woman peering at me through round spectacles. She helped Shan ease me to my feet and into the room at the top of the stairs. A small furnace made the place humid as a hot summer noon. Tools were scattered on a table and jars ranged on shelves rising over it. A green cloth covered something on the table. I didn't have to look to know what.

"This is Cade, the Finder I told you about," Shan said. "He's hurt. Cade, this is Caron. She was my governess, and now she's our scholar. You can trust her. She'll know what to do," Shan added with such relief in her voice that it dawned on me she'd been worried.

I looked at the cut again. Was it that bad?

While Shan gabbled, Caron helped me onto a bench. I gritted my teeth as she pulled my bloody shirt away from my ribs. She squinted through the tear, ripped the cloth so she could see better, and clicked her tongue. "Get water and a clean cloth, Shan. How did this happen?" She frowned at Shan, who hurried around to do as she'd been told. One side of Shan's apron was smeared with something dark. It took me a moment to realize it was my blood.

"Something unexpected came up," Shan said.

"I'd say so," Caron said. "Did you get the last two stones?"

Shan handed her a cloth and set a basin of water on the bench. She pulled the half-moon heart stone from an inner apron pocket and showed it to Caron. "Just this one. Can you use it or one of the others to heal his cut?"

I started to tell Shan to get the stone away from me, but Caron wiped a wet cloth across my side, and I sucked my breath in and held it against the flood of pain.

"It's not deep," Caron said. "I imagine it hurts though."

"Not much," I said through clenched teeth.

Caron smiled. "I'll close it as well as I can and bandage it. You should be fine." Before I could stop her, she pinched the edges of the wound together, took the half-moon stone, and ran it over my side.

Warmth poured through me, and the pain went away. My head swam, and then filled with the faint tinkle of chimes. The music was beautiful. I strained to hear it. Just as I realized I wanted to listen to it forever, it stopped.

My fuzzy vision focused on Caron, who had lifted the stone away. Her face wrinkled in concern. I reached for the half-moon stone, then realized what I was doing and yanked my hand back.

"What's the matter?" Shan stared at me over Caron's shoulder.

"He's just a little stone sick. He shouldn't stay here too long." Caron looked at my ribs and raised an eyebrow. "The cut's healed though. I don't believe he even needs a bandage. Interesting. I've never healed a Finder before. Their greater sensitivity to heart stones must make the healing more effective."

I twisted to look where the knife had caught me and saw only a faint, pink line. I touched it gently. No pain at all. "How did you do that?"

"A heart stone fixes a body's disrupted energy, and lets it heal itself," Caron said. "That's what you feel as a Finder, and the resulting sense of well-being is why Finders are so drawn to the stones. In touch with a heart stone, they forget all their pains and problems."

For the first time, I realized how strong Mum must have been to even talk to Roth and me, much less go to the Long Street shrine while holding the triangular stone. If Beam hadn't nabbed her, she'd have left it in the shrine. I was sure of it. I felt an even wilder than usual flood of bitterness at the lie that Mum and other Finders had to be locked away for everyone else's safety. When Beam stopped Mum, all he'd done was give the miners another worker for their mines, one they wouldn't have had if Mum had put the stone in the shrine and shed the Finder's gift.

Caron handed the half-moon stone to Shan. I followed it with my eyes, and Caron had to nudge me to make me take the man's shirt she was offering. I shrugged it on over my shredded one. It was a smock really, meant to cover a good shirt and keep it from dirt and damage. A scattering of burn holes pockmarked one sleeve.

I needed to get my mind off heart stones. "Where are we besides the city drains?"

"In a blocked-up cellar under Syndicate House," Shan said.

"Tricky gods," I said.

A rumble rolled overhead. The floor shook, and the tools rattled right along with my heart.

"Aren't you afraid of the cellar collapsing on you?" I looked up at cracked beams.

Caron shrugged. "We need Governor Barth's big stone to cloak the presence of ours."

"Who's he?" a man's voice asked. "And why is he wearing my smock?" A young man scowled in the doorway. He looked older than Roth, but not by much. He wore an embroidered shirt with a fancy gold pin closing the collar—the rose of the jewelers' syndicate, one of the two groups who profited most from the slave work of Finders digging heart stones.

I felt like someone had just thrown a hunk of spoiled meat into the room.

"His shirt was ruined when he helped me take a stone today," Shan said. "This is Cade, our new Finder."

The jeweler's scowl deepened. "The one who helped catch Jem. Are you sure he won't turn us in?"

Us? This jeweler was part of Shan's gang of thieves?

"He's fine, Keled," Shan said. "Cade, this is Keled, our glassworker. He makes the stones to replace the ones we steal."

"Some Finders betray people hiding stones." Keled eyed me narrowly. "Someone makes them, or they want money, or they just want the stones for themselves."

"I'd never do that." I closed and opened my fists, as insulted at a jeweler accusing me of greed as a cat would be if a hog said it was dirty. "You don't know me."

"I know Jem, and I know he's in jail and headed for the mine, and I know you put him there." Keled set a loaf of bread and jug of ale on the table next to the cloth under which Shan had slipped the half-moon stone.

The gesture led my attention right to where it had been straying anyway. Eyes on the cloth, I rose and took a step toward it. One peek wouldn't hurt. "It was a mistake. I thought Jem was just thieving."

"So you say." Keled moved between me and the stones.

"Yeah, I do. Get out of my way."

When he was too slow to move, I drove my fist into his belly. With an "oof," he doubled over and hugged his gut. I pushed past him, but Keled lunged, wrapped his arms around me, and lifted me off the ground. I went limp, but like Roth, he knew that trick, so I kicked back at his shin. His arms tightened.

Shan scrambled in front of us. "Stop it, both of you," she cried. "Cade, what's wrong with you?"

"It's the stones," Keled said. "He wants them."

Gods help me. He was right. I did.

"Let him go, Keled," Shan said.

I felt how much he hated to do it in the slow way he loosened his grip, but it seemed like Shan was the boss here. He moved next to me, straightened his fancy shirt, and stood ready to grab again if I breathed the wrong way. I kept hold of myself but only by a hair. "I just want to see them," I said. "Then I'll go."

Caron lifted the cloth off ten heart stones set in a circle and nudged the half-moon one into line with them.

Keled followed me and stood close by, tidying the tools while I regarded the stones.

They looked like they were just lying there, but they pulsed with life and energy, each one a little different. The stone Shan and I had taken from Hathen was there, giving off a throb I felt in my belly. Next to it sat one matching the fake in the jeweled box Wilder had held to test me. Its feel was tighter and faster.

If I'd thought about it ahead of time, I'd have guessed a bunch of stones would draw me in even more strongly than a single one, but that turned out not to be so. Like Keled said, I wanted them, but eleven stones knocking together made me feel worse, not better.

Still, I stretched a finger toward a long, thin one. Keled gripped my wrist. "Try to touch them again, and I'll stick your hand in the furnace."

I pulled free of Keled's grip and wiped my palms on my trousers. "I've been letting Shan walk away with them. I'm not piggish enough to keep them. They just rattle me."

"Jem managed fine," Keled said.

"Jem couldn't come in here," Shan said sharply. "And he lost his head in that last house we robbed. That's why he was caught."

Keled stomped off and flung himself onto the bench.

I turned back to the table and frowned at the circle of stones. "Is this how they go on the temple altar?"

"I'm not sure," Caron said. "The old scholars say that at midnight on New Year's Eve, they have to be on the altar, balancing one another. I've been trying to figure out how to arrange them, and as best I can interpret the scholars, this is what they suggest."

"They're not what I'd call balanced," I said. "They're fighting one another."

"What?" she said.

"They each feel different." I moved my hand over the stones, then curled my fingers away. "The bigger ones give off more power, but their shape changes their feel too. Right now...well, arranged like this they sort of hurt."

Caron swapped an oval stone for a tiny one. "Is that better?"

"I don't know. I don't think so."

She fiddled some more, but the stones still clanged.

"Maybe we need all twelve," I said. "Or maybe they only balance at the temple because it's at the world's center."

"Or maybe you're just bad at this," Keled said.

"You wouldn't know, would you?" I said. "You can't feel them at all."

Shan rolled her eyes. "We should be going, Cade." She took off her blood stained apron and handed it to Caron.

"Make sure he hasn't tucked one of those stones in his pocket," Keled said.

"I'd never do that." I smiled nastily. "Only rich folks hoard them. You know, the ones jewelers sell to and get rich themselves."

Keled flushed but said nothing.

"We all have to trust one another." Caron draped Shan's apron over her arm and looked steadily at Keled and then at me. "Jeweler and Finder, we work together, or anyone not rich enough to own a heart stone will suffer."

"Fine," I said. "Let's go, Shan."

We slogged back through the storeroom.

"What's with Keled?" I asked as we waded back through the drains.

Something green and scaly that wasn't a fish swam past and vanished in the dark. I moved closer to the wall.

"Keled's father is the jeweler who owned Jem as his appraiser." Shan's voice echoed in the tunnel.

"Nobody 'owned' Jem," I said.

"True. Bad choice of words. Keled was horrified by the way his father treated Jem. I went to the shop because I'd heard there was a Finder there, and I wound up with Keled willing to make the fake stones I needed too."

"I'll bet he'd been making them for his father to sell," I said.

"It doesn't matter," Shan said. "Keled's the one who got Jem away. The news that Jem had been recaptured just about killed him."

She loosened the grate, climbed to the street, and took my hand to haul me up. I thought about Keled while I put the grate back and couldn't help feeling a little ashamed of myself for picking at him. It wouldn't have been easy for him to walk away from his family to help a Finder, especially when Shan intended to steal stones from people like him.

Shan shook out her skirts. "My father expects me home, expected me before this really." She wrapped her arms around herself.

"Why go home?" I asked. "You don't have to. There's an old lady who lives near me who'd probably let you stay with her."

Shan smiled crookedly. "He's my only family. You know how that is."

I did, but no one in my family scared me enough to make me hide from them. Shan was smart and brave, and she cared about other people. She deserved better.

"Father wants me tomorrow morning too," Shan said, "but I'll find out where the Malels live and meet you here at mid-day. There's no point in leaving a fake stone now that time's so short, so we can take the stone on the first trip. That'll give Caron the rest of tomorrow and all of New Year's Eve to get the arrangement right."

I ducked my head so she wouldn't see me flinch at the mention of the Malels' stone. Yes, they probably had one, but what if they didn't? I'd told Keled that I'd never keep a stone because that would condemn everyone else, but lying to Shan about having found the twelfth stone wouldn't do everyone else much good at New Year either.

"I think I'll look for more stones now, just in case the Malels don't have one." I left her, still brushing her clothes and hair into shape.

I was on the Inner Circle, and that was as likely a place to look as any, so I kept walking, rubbing at the place on my side where the thief cut me. Maybe being knifed should have scared me more, but what I really worried about was how I'd wanted the stones in the governor's cellar, wanted them badly enough to slug Keled to get near them.

I resisted, I told myself. *I didn't touch them, and I didn't take them.*

Ahead was a house whose front gates were open. I hurried toward it. A wagon stood in the courtyard, and the place was full of men unloading poles, coils of rope, and rolls of green striped canvas that I recognized as tent pieces. This house's owner must be planning to hold his New Year party in his garden. The only person I saw in the courtyard was a bent-backed old man shoveling horse droppings into a wheelbarrow. The knees of his trousers looked permanently stained green. A gardener, I guessed.

A man who'd been out of sight behind the wagon came around it and reached for another bunch of poles.

Tricky gods. Roth.

I dove behind the open gate and peeked through its bars. So maybe I hid from someone in my family sometimes after all.

As Roth pulled the poles out of the wagon and hoisted them onto one shoulder, the ground roared and shook so hard I had to hold onto the gate to stay upright. Roth staggered sideways, and the poles crashed onto the cobblestones. When the earth steadied again, he scrambled after them and started gathering them up.

"You clumsy oaf!" A man in a bright blue brocade coat ran into sight, waving his arms. His trousers were a startling yellow silk and snug as sausage casing. He was dressed more or less like a monkey I'd seen with traveling players. "If those poles are so much as scratched, I'll have them for free."

Roth kept his head down, but his ears turned red. He grabbed the last one. "They're fine, sir."

"You'd better hope so," the man said.

Roth carried the poles around to the side of the house with the man right behind him, still yelling. The man was undoubtedly the house's master. He was also king of the ugly toads, and I was sick of people like him dishing out abuse to people like Roth.

I strode into the courtyard. "I'm with the workers out back," I told the gardener.

"They're trampling my flowers," the old guy wailed, "and when I told them to keep off, they sent me away to mind the gate." He pounded the tip of the shovel onto the cobblestones. A hunk of manure slid off.

"I'll tell them to be careful," I said.

I side-stepped the horse dung and was already around the corner of the house when the gardener called, "Tell them to mind the flowers."

I followed men's voices to the back yard. Like the other yards in the city, this one had undoubtedly been flat to start with. But the gardener had been at work, probably for years, moving dirt around and reshaping it. The center of the yard was hollowed out, and from there, it slanted up to bushes, with spring flowers blooming in a rainbow of colors between graveled paths. It was very pretty. No wonder the owner wanted to hold his party there.

The problem was so many flowers didn't leave much room for a tent. Poles had been set up for the tent's back half, and canvas had been unrolled and draped over them, but they were tight up against a flower bed. Even from where I lurked, I saw crushed flowers.

With tent poles lying by their feet, Roth and some other workers waited while the master shouted at a man whose back was to me, Roth's foreman probably. "Tell your men to get it away from the flowers. Put the pole there." The master pointed to a spot a few yards away.

The foreman turned and snapped his fingers at Roth. "You heard him. Put the pole up over there."

Well, well. Now that I saw the foreman's face, I knew him. It was Faldor, who'd hit me. When I'd worried about Roth still working for him, Roth said he'd changed jobs. I guess not.

"The ground there's not deep enough to hold a pole, sir." Roth's face was flushed.

"You mean you're too lazy to push it in," the master said.

"If you can't do what you're told, I can't be expected to pay you," Faldor said.

"It won't be solid there," Roth said.

Faldor shoved his face close to Roth's, though he had to bend his head back and look up to do it. "You're fired, you useless lout."

It was all I could do not to run down the hill, pick up a tent pole, and beat him with it.

Instead, Faldor was the one who grabbed a pole and carried it to the spot the master had chosen. He drove the pointed end into the ground. The master came to lean on the pole too, and they tried to twist it deeper.

Something rattled and squeaked behind me, and the smell of manure crept up my nose. The gardener halted his wheelbarrow next to me, let go of the handles, and straightened as much as he could. "My flowers!" Arms outstretched as if to rescue a child in danger, he shuffled down the hillside and across to the ruined flowerbed.

For the idea they put in my head at that instant, I'd love the tricky gods forever.

I seized the wheelbarrow and trundled it up a path leading behind the row of bushes at the garden's upper end. Storage sheds and a wood pile hid between the bushes and the wall, and so did another pile of manure and rotting garbage.

The gardener had left the shovel in the wheelbarrow. The part of the tent canvas that had already been put up hid the master and Faldor from me, but I could hear Faldor swearing, so I figured I had time to add a few more shovelfuls of muck to the barrow.

Then I steered it to the top of the steep path leading down into the back of the tent. I looked to be sure Roth was out of the way. He and the other workers had stepped aside and stood near where the gardener knelt. Roth sank down to sit with his hands on his knees.

I gave the barrow a hard shove. It rolled down the path, picking up speed. Just before it reached the tent canvas, the ground rumbled and shook so hard that I fell on my backside.

"Watch it, you fool!" the master cried.

The back of the tent swayed, then collapsed when the loaded wheelbarrow drove its way under the canvas. The master and Faldor both shrieked as canvas fell, trapping them with a barrow of manure. Judging by the way the bumps under the canvas moved, the barrow tipped over just as it reached them.

I felt like a general who'd won a war.

I ran toward the garden wall behind Roth. The flower beds there had been built so high that the wall reached only to my chest. I hauled myself up onto it, then looked back to enjoy myself one more time.

Faldor and the master still thrashed around under the canvas. Roth, the other workers, and even the gardener were howling with laughter. I smiled at my brother's back.

Roth raised his hand to scratch his neck.

I stared. No. I must be seeing wrong. Roth's neck was covered in a thick rash.

When I still didn't, he touched my shoulder lightly. "Don't worry. We have to go, but not without Mum. After all, we know where to find her."

My gaze met his. His brown eyes were cold and hard as the frozen mud in the street. I started stuffing clothes in my carry bag.

13. FOR FAMILY

Would you know what lurks in the dark? Go look.—Sig, the shadow god

Roth had fever.

My momentum carried me off the wall and down into the passageway a good three yards below. My mind filled with the image of the scarlet rash on Roth's neck, and my gut flooded with terror. People died from that fever. I had to get back to Roth.

I jumped and reached for the top of the garden wall, but it was too far above my head. I looked around. One end of the passage was closed, so I ran the other way into a tangle of alleys that got narrower and narrower. I hit a dead end, turned back, ran a different way, hit what looked like the same dead end. My heart thudded. Sweat ran down my back. Finally, I burst out of the maze, looking frantically around at a street I didn't know. I ran to the corner. Two blocks away, I glimpsed a house with glass windows that had to be on the Inner Circle. I pelted that way and then around the curve of the Inner Circle. Where was the house? Had I gotten so turned around that I'd run the wrong way?

There! I ran through the gate and around the house. Both the house's master and the gardener were gone, but Faldor's whole crew looked up when I tore down the path. They were still struggling to get the tent posts up. I turned in a circle, scanning the yard for the one person I wanted to see and not finding him.

"Here! I know you." Faldor grabbed my shoulder and spun me roughly. "You're the mouthy little one. I just threw your lazy brother out, and I'll toss you onto your ear too if you don't get out of here."

"Roth's gone?" I panted.

"I just said that. Now get out." He shoved me, and I staggered back up the path.

Roth must be on his way home. I headed there too, watching for Roth, but not seeing him. Could he be sick enough to have wandered off? No, surely he'd be home when I got there.

But he wasn't. The house was so empty, it echoed. I tried to make my brain stop churning and think straight and was deciding whether to go out looking when the door opened and Roth dragged in. His face was gray, and his shoulders sagged like an old man's.

"You're sick!" I jumped to take his arm and help him to a stool.

"Don't worry. It's nothing." His breath wheezed. "Maybe you could unroll my pallet though. I think I have to lie down." He laid his head on the table and worked his feet against one another to pry his shoes off.

I grabbed his rolled-up bedding and shook it so the straw stuffing rustled into place. I waited for him to get up and move to it, but he didn't. Instead he unbuttoned his shirt. I caught my breath. His chest, stomach, and back were covered with rash—red bumps, some of them already oozing pus.

"The best thing happened today," he mumbled. "You know Faldor?"

I gripped his elbow and levered him off the stool. The heat rolled off him. "The weasel who hit me."

"He and this house owner were both being horses' behinds, and one of those strange shakes happened." He shuffled toward his pallet, leaning so heavily on my shoulder that I staggered. "The tent collapsed on them, and a wheelbarrow of dung got knocked loose and tipped all over them. The owner had been swanning around in new clothes, and they were covered in it." He laughed weakly as I lowered him onto the pallet, pulled off his trousers, and drew up the blanket.

His eyes closed, and he sucked in a noisy breath. His smile faded. "Faldor fired me."

I patted his shoulder awkwardly, then looked at my hand. What if I caught what he had? I quickly wiped my hand on my trousers. I'd wash it, I told myself. I couldn't get sick. Roth needed me. "You'll get another job. It's all right."

"I'm just...so tired." He shuddered. "I'm cold."

I pulled his blanket up higher. He felt hot to me, but his teeth chattered. His eyelids lowered. He wasn't asleep, but he sure wasn't awake.

I sat on my stool, staring at Roth's face. It was flushed now, and his eyes moved under the closed lids. In the distance, the ground rumbled, rattling the dishes, but Roth's eyes stayed shut. Oh gods. He was really sick.

I got the rag we used to bathe, poured water into a basin, and dipped the rag. His sweat gave off a strange sour tang. When I wiped it off his face, he turned away, muttering. He felt hot right through the wet rag. If steam had risen off him, I wouldn't have been surprised. I pulled down his blanket and wiped his arms and chest too. His hands flapped, and he tried to push me away, but he couldn't. Roth had been strong enough to hold me still while Mum sewed up a gash in my thigh, but at the moment, he couldn't push my hands away.

The rag was warm, so I dipped it again and wiped at his chest some more, then covered him up, and went back to sit on my stool.

I was hungry, but I couldn't leave Roth long enough to go all the way to the market. I'd eaten my noon bread and cheese, but his was still in his trouser pocket. Maybe I should try to feed it to him? I looked at it and then at my unconscious brother. I set aside most of the bread in case he woke up later, but I ate the cheese. What Roth needed was probably something like soup. I knew how to make it if I had onions and barley and maybe some meat, but I didn't, and we didn't own a brazier, so I couldn't have cooked it even if I had Elgar's warehouse full of stuff.

I filled a cup with water, raised his shoulder, and held it to his mouth. "Roth? Wake up and drink." I shook him a little. "Roth?"

His eyes flew open. "No!" One flailing arm knocked the cup away, flinging an arc of water across his blanket and mine. The knuckles of his other hand whacked me in the mouth. "They're coming!" he cried. "Go away! Fire! Oh fire!" He rolled away, then lay panting on his side like he'd moved all he could.

For a moment, I couldn't stir. I'd never seen Roth like this, out of control, less than logical, lost in a world I couldn't imagine.

"Roth, it's all right." I touched his shoulder, and when I was sure he wouldn't swing his fists like I was attacking him, I rolled him back onto his pallet. "It's all right."

"All right," he mumbled. "All right." His eyes closed.

I sat back on my heels and sucked salty blood where a tooth had cut my lip. Oh gods. What was I going to do? I got up and washed my hands, then sat to watch him.

Day wore into night. I lay down on my pallet, but Roth kept floundering around, kicking off his blanket and muttering with fever dreams. Then I'd get up, wipe the stinking sweat off him, and cover him up again. Every so often, the earth shook and rumbled. I must have fallen asleep after a while because one of the rumbles woke me. I rolled over to face Roth and found him still covered from the last time I'd gotten up. He wasn't moving. My heart lurched. Oh gods. Had he died while I slept? I scrambled on hands and knees from my pallet to his, put out my hand, and touched him. If he'd been any hotter, my fingers would have blistered.

I got another cup of water and held it to his cracked lips. "Roth?"

He moaned.

I trickled a little water on his mouth. "Roth?" I shook him. "Roth!"

After a moment, I let go of him. He wasn't fighting me. He wasn't doing anything.

"If you die," I said, "I'll run around doing whatever I want."

Roth didn't so much as stir.

Everything else I did seemed about as useful as my threat. I wiped him down and watched him. Morning came. I ate the bread I'd set aside because it was turning to rock anyway. I had to soak it in water to make it chewable even for me, and Roth looked like he'd never eat again. Even after soaking, I choked and could only eat when I turned away from my brother. It scraped my throat all the way down.

I dragged my sleeve under my nose. I stared through the window at storm clouds boiling across the sky and thought about Roth showing me how to blow gently on the tinder when I lit a fire, Roth telling off a bully who'd come after me when I was six, Roth letting me sleep with him the night Dad died. I thought about being alone.

When it came close to mid-day, I finally decided I had to go meet Shan and look for the Malels' house. If I got hold of Mum, I'd ask Granny to take her in until Roth was better. That way Mum wouldn't catch fever. And surely the Malels would have the twelfth heart stone. Putting the heart stones in the temple was the only thing I could think of that would help Roth for sure, assuming he lived until New Year of course. I covered him up and went out.

On my way to the Inner Circle, I passed carry bag laden walkers and lots of carriages and carts on their way out of town, looking for safe ground. Supposedly, things would be worst here at the world's center, so you couldn't blame them. Just before I got to the alcove where I was meeting Shan, I saw the Watch lifting a man's body into the corpse cart. My heart beat so fast, I was dizzy.

Shan was peeking out of the alcove when I got there. "You're late. But no matter. I found out where the Malels live."

My dizziness vanished. "We're still looking for my mum too."

"Agreed." She led me away from the governor's and through an area that was mostly fancy shops. From up ahead came the sound of angry voices and then a sharp crack of wood. We rounded a corner to see a crowd of people surging around a jeweler's shop. Two men in the front drove a bench through the closed shutter. One of the men scrambled through the window, and others poured in after him.

"Do they have heart stones?" shouted someone from the back of the crowd. "For the love of the gods, throw at least one of them out."

A pair of Watchmen pounded into the street and toward the crowd swinging their clubs. Then, behind us, a whistle blew. The Crows were about to join the fight. This was a jeweler after all and under their protection. We'd be in trouble if we got caught in this mess.

I pushed Shan into a side street, and we hustled out of sight though I could still hear shouting.

She was pale and breathing hard. "I hear things like that are happening all over the city. This way. We're not far from the house the Malels are renting."

We crept into a passage that led to a house's side gate. I peered through into a narrow yard full of overgrown grass. The shutters were open both upstairs and down, and the quiver of a heart stone rippled on the air. That was good. Shan would have her twelfth stone, so I didn't have to feel guilty for lying to her. So now, all I needed to know was if Mum was hidden in that house.

Shan tried the latch, and the gate creaked open. She tsked. "They're as trusting as two-year-olds. Someone needs to tell them an unlocked gate in the city begs thieves to come calling."

She skimmed over the grass. I followed her through a small door into what I now recognized as servant quarters.

I looked down the hallway, and my heart squeezed. Not a single door was barred. But maybe Mum was working in the heartroom. I slipped past Shan, crept quickly to the entrance, and peeked around the screen. Tables were arranged all around the room, set with plates and silverware and goblets. Lilacs were massed on the altar. The house was ready for its New Year party, but the only person in the heartroom was a man sitting at a small table in a corner, looking over papers and sipping wine. He wore a dark velvet surcoat that made his white-blond hair glow in contrast. Malel, I guessed, with a surge of loathing. I wanted to punch him in the gut until he spewed up his wine.

Instead I pulled back into the hallway and leaned against the wall. Where was Mum? Could Malel have rented her to a jeweler? Could she be at a warehouse, checking his shipments? Could he have sent her back to the mine?

Shan patted my slumping shoulder. "Sorry." Then she raised an eyebrow at me. I stared at her stupidly. "Where's the heart stone?" she asked.

Yes. The heart stone. I had to go on no matter how awful I felt. For Roth's sake, I needed to at least find the heart stone. I couldn't lose both him and Mum.

"Not here." I turned slowly and stopped facing a stairway. Wisps of warmth drifted down it. "There."

Shan hurried to the stairs. Two maids were talking in the upstairs hall, and we waited until they'd gone down another stairway before I pointed out what I thought was the right room. Shan listened at the door, then silently cracked it to peek inside. She slipped through, and I went after her.

For someone who was here only on a visit, this house's mistress had a lot of stuff. Clothes and chests and jewel boxes littered the room. I stood in the middle, wondering desperately where Mum was and how Roth was doing.

"Cade?" Shan sounded like she'd said my name more than once.

I dragged my mind back to what I was doing. "That way, I think." I nodded toward a second door.

Shan opened it to show more heaps of clothes and jewel boxes. "This woman's governess did not sufficiently stress tidiness." Shan plunged into the mess.

I drifted to the doorway, and as I watched her, my hand came to rest on a silk scarf thrown over a chair back. Something hard lay underneath. I lifted the silk.

Caught on the chair back was a necklace with a triangular heart stone.

For an instant, I thought I was imagining it. The last time I'd seen this stone, I'd put it in Mum's hand and sent her to the mine. I blinked and the stone was still there. A tempting thought crept into my head. I'd hurt Mum with that stone, but maybe I could use it now to help Roth.

The triangular stone dangled from the clasp on one end of its chain. I reached, hesitated, and wrapped my hand in the scarf. Then I freed the stone from the chain and slid it out of sight into my pocket.

"Are you sure the stone's here, Cade?" Shan's voice was muffled in the pile of shimmering blue silk she was lifting off a chest.

"Now that you ask, I don't think it is." I dropped the scarf back on the chair. The stone sang in my pocket.

Shan turned to frown at me.

"The feeling's faded." My heart pounded. Could she hear the lie in my voice? "Maybe it was here when we came into the house, and then the mistress went out wearing it."

Shan came to stand with one hand braced on either side of the dressing room door. Her forehead creased. "We're running out of time. The calendar changes at midnight tomorrow. We need to find another stone."

"I can't look now," I said. "My brother has fever."

"I'm sorry," Shan said, "but our finding another stone is what he needs too."

I should give her the triangular stone. I'd called people selfish for keeping stones. I'd told Keled I'd never keep one. But Roth had fever, and a heart stone in our house would make him better. Besides, the stone was mine. I'd found it, and Mum had paid for it with her freedom. I had a right to use it for Roth.

What a miner's thought, jeered a voice in my head.

There had to be another way, one that would let me keep Mum's stone and still help Shan.

"Shan," I said, "what about Governor Barth's stone?"

Shan frowned out the window toward where you could see the roof of Syndicate House not too far away. The sounds of the chaos by the jeweler's flooded through the open window—people screaming, more Crows' whistles.

"You said it's guarded," I said, "but maybe your friend can help you."

She let out a long breath. "I suppose it will have to be that one."

"Will you be able to find it without me?" I started toward the hallway.

"Yes. I know where it is."

I was so relieved I was almost happy. Shan would have enough heart stones to use in the temple. It didn't matter if I kept this one. We slipped into the hallway and had crept down the first few steps when men's voices came from the servants' hall below.

"The master wants that grass cut," one man said.

"There's riot in the street," the second one said.

"So lock that gate," the first man said.

Shan plucked at my shirt to draw me back, and we tiptoed to a different stairway. At its foot, Shan pushed open a door, peeked around it, and ran out into an empty stable yard. She was urging me across to a wall that looked climbable when I spotted it—a lean-to built against the side of the house, one with bars on the window and door.

With Shan hissing after me, I ran toward it. I heaved at the bar on the door. It stuck, then came loose so suddenly I staggered back. The door swung open on its own. I stumbled to the doorway and peered into the dusky little room. At first, all I saw was the cot. Then I saw the woman huddled in the corner, rocking and singing to herself.

Mum.

I rushed to her and crouched to fling my arms around her. "Mum! Mum!" I was laughing and crying all at once. She was here! I'd found her!

It took me a moment to realize she wasn't hugging me back. Instead, she shrugged like I was annoying her. I backed off and took a good look.

Her hair was filthy and tangled. Her face—turned away from the light in the doorway—was incurious about anything outside her head. As far as I could tell, she was as interested in me as she was in the fly buzzing over the abandoned plate of ham scraps.

"Mum," I urged. "Mum, get up. I'm going to get you out of here."

"Let me help." Shan looked appalled, but she took Mum's other elbow, and we got her to her feet.

Mum let us guide her out of the dirty little hut, docile as a lamb to the slaughter. "Stones?" she asked. Something caught in my throat. She was probably used to being brought out to check whether heart stones were genuine so Malel could make money off them.

Shan paused in the shadow of the hut and looked around.

"She can't climb the wall," I said.

"I know," Shan said. "We'll have to go back out the side gate."

We started toward the corner of the house, but Mum was dragging. She patted my chest. My heart leapt. She knew me after all.

"Let me touch the stone," she croaked.

So it wasn't me she recognized, but the heart stone in my pocket. I glanced at Shan, but she didn't seem to realize Mum meant a stone I was hiding.

"Stones aren't good for you, Mum," I said. "You're going to get well again."

Mum moaned.

Shan darted ahead and peered around the corner, then beckoned us to her. When we drew even with her, she signaled us to wait.

I heard a scythe snicking through grass. The sound grew fainter.

Shan held us in place a moment more, then grabbed Mum's arm and hustled her across the side yard toward the gate. The man scything the grass was moving away, his back toward us. Beyond the yard wall, the riot near the jeweler's shop had grown louder, and a man flashed past the gate, running down the side passage. Trouble was coming closer. The grass cutter looked up nervously.

I hauled on the gate, but it didn't budge. To my horror, I saw that a padlock now hung from it.

Shan must have seen it too. She produced her ring of tools and set to work, hands flying, while I held onto Mum.

"The stone," Mum said. "Please."

"What are you doing?" The grass cutter had seen us.

Shan popped the padlock and opened the gate. I dragged Mum through. Shan took her other arm and we ran, Mum's toes scraping the dirt between us.

The grass cutter burst out of the yard, scythe held high. "Help! Thieves!"

We yanked Mum along, my arms nearly tearing from their sockets, for all that Mum was way too thin for her dirty clothes. We stumbled out into the street to see a crowd boiling toward us, driven by club-wielding Watchmen and Crows. We started to back up, but the grass cutter was there. I grabbed Mum's arm to run across the street before the mob was on us. Mum seemed to come awake to our danger, because she too broke into a run, but her toe caught on a cobble. With a cry, she slipped from my grip.

A mass of running rioters swept over us.

14. PROBLEMS WITH STONES

Life grows wide in the small space between a book's covers.—
Lerned, the wise god

A wild-eyed man rammed into me, and I went down. Someone tripped over me and fell. Arms flung up to protect my head, I crawled on my elbows, desperate to get out of the way.

A pool of space lay at the base of a statue that turned out to be Ras the Trickster. I huddled into it and pulled myself to my feet. Watchmen and Crows thundered past on both sides, chasing the escaping crowd. Neither Mum nor Shan was anywhere in sight even when I climbed up on Ras to see better. He grinned at me like this was just his normal mischief. I wanted to smack his teeth out.

The mob moved on. I jumped to the ground and started searching, running from side street to passage to alley. I looked into every yard I could, behind every water barrel and bush. Finally, I had to brace my hands on my knees and take a moment to get my breath back. Despair burned like a lump of hot charcoal in my chest.

From the next street, a Watchman's whistle blew. "Curfew now!" he bellowed. "Everyone off the streets."

The sky was darkening, but it was still too early for curfew. The Watch must be afraid of the mob.

I rocked from foot to foot, trying to figure out what to do. The stone in my pocket felt warm against my leg. All right. One thing at least was clear. I had to get that stone home to Roth.

"Curfew now!" The Watchman was closer. "Everyone off the street under pain of arrest."

Maybe Shan had Mum. I held onto that flicker of hope and began slipping toward home. Twice I had to duck out of the way of Watch patrols clearing the streets, and it was close to dark by the time I ran into our house.

Roth lay exactly where I'd left him, his chest barely lifting and falling. Should I tuck the stone under his blanket? No, it would work best in the center of the house. I crept under the table and, using my shirtsleeve to shield my hand, I wedged the stone into one of the leg braces.

In the distance, a rumble started, then grew louder and louder. The ground shook hard enough that one of our two plates fell off the shelf and broke in half.

A boom rattled the air.

Heart pounding, I grabbed the edge of the skittering table. Both my hands and the ground stopped trembling, and, after a moment, I heard people shouting in the street. I took a last look at Roth who hadn't stirred and went out to see what was happening.

Curfew or no curfew, all the neighbors were out, gibbering to one another and gaping at a house up the lane. A crack had opened in the earth, and one wall of the house had broken off and slid in. A table teetered on the crack's edge. The woman who lived there was in the street, crying in the arms of her half-grown daughter.

I followed the line of the crack. It zigzagged toward our house, then veered away, down another lane. Our house and the ones connected to it were untouched.

The woman who lived next door to the broken house spoke shrilly. "I heard a bunch of carters were going to march to Syndicate House and demand Governor Barth do something, or that the syndicates choose a different governor."

"What do you imagine Barth can do?" a tinsmith from the next lane asked. "What can a governor do against weather and illness? If the calendar change really is causing this, there's nothing anyone can do." He wiped his hand over his trembling mouth.

"There's heart stones," the woman said.

"You have one?" the tinsmith said. "I don't."

"I'm going to tell my man we have to get the kids out of the city before New Year," the woman said.

"Curfew!" A pair of Watchmen trotted down the lane, probably drawn by the noise. "Everyone inside!"

One of them turned pale at the sight of the crack, but the other herded people to their doors.

I couldn't take a chance on being arrested, so I went back in the house and closed the door.

It would be all right, I told myself. Mum was probably with Shan. And tomorrow, Shan would steal Governor Barth's stone, and she and Caron and Keled would put all the stones in the temple. Everything would be fine.

I went to look at Roth. In the twilight, his face looked gray. He'd be better soon, I thought. It was just taking time.

A storm blew in, blotting out the moon. Rain beat on the roof and dripped into the bucket once I put it in the right place, but at least the earth-splitting rumbles sounded far away.

I slept for a while until a blast of thunder kicked me awake. I crawled to Roth's pallet. When I touched him, he was still hot.

Lightning flashed between the shutters, and thunder crashed again. When I went to the window, rain rushed down the lane in a muddy river. The triangular stone sang to me from under the table. Was it helping Roth? Was Mum all right?

Struggling to ignore the stone, I slid back under my blanket, and when I opened my eyes again, the rain had stopped and sweltering heat had oozed into the house. It was New Year's Eve. At midnight tonight, the calendar would change to the year 4000. I hoped Shan was ready.

I scrambled to Roth's side. He hadn't moved. I reached out a trembling hand and felt his forehead. Sweet gods, it was cool. I yanked his blanket down. His rash was fading. I sat back on my heels and closed my eyes.

Then I took a deep breath. I had things to do. Roth would be hungry when he woke up, and I was starving now. I'd go to market. Then I'd leave food out for Roth and go look for Shan in the hideout under Syndicate House. She could tell me where Mum was. As a matter of fact, maybe Mum was there. I climbed into my clothes.

Outside, I eyed the crack in the ground. Two kids from the next lane were dropping rocks in it and listening for them to hit bottom. As far as I could hear, they fell forever. I turned the other way. The air was hot and wet as soup, and the lane was sticky with mud, but Granny still sat on her stool. The skin under her eyes looked bruised.

"You been sick, Granny?"

"I have, but overnight I got a lot better." She smiled up at me, shading her eyes from the sun's glare with her hand.

That was my doing, I thought with satisfaction. Judging by how that crack had turned away, the heart stone at our house protected the ones attached to it too.

"Can I get you something at the market?" I asked.

"No. I've not been hungry, so I have enough."

I headed for the market. On my way, I passed knots of people loaded with carry bags and heading out of town. From their talk, the cracking earth had pushed them over the edge. Weather and fever were one thing. You always had those, though not so bad. But when the ground started swallowing houses, that was another. If I hadn't known about Shan's plan, I'd have panicked too. Of course to succeed, she had to have stolen Governor Barth's heart stone. Shan was good at thieving. I gave a half smile. If Roth were awake, he'd pass out again at the idea I'd been spending my days with someone I complimented by thinking they were good at thieving.

As I drew near the market, my skin started itching like ants were crawling inside my clothes. I paused at the end of the lane, my eyes on the temple. A bunch of heart stones were in there. Caron must be working on arranging them. Maybe Shan was too, and I could ask about Mum.

I'd shop first though, which wouldn't take me long because not many people were there, and some of the market stalls were closed. I still had most of Shan's money, but I bought cheap food anyway because neither Roth nor I had a job now.

When I had two days' supply, I waited until no one was looking and crept into the temple ruins. I had a bare glimpse of Shan and Caron at the altar before someone grabbed my arm and spun me around. My package of bread and cheese bounced on the temple floor.

"Oh," Keled said. "It's you."

He let go of me, and I turned to see Shan holding out her skirts, trying to hide what Caron was doing. She laughed and let them fall.

"We might have known you'd show up," Shan said. "I suppose every Finder in the city feels this."

"Do you know what happened to my mum yesterday?" I asked.

Her smile vanished. "I thought you had her."

My throat spasmed. Mum was still out there.

"Cade, can you look at these?" Caron said.

Keled released me but stayed close enough that his breath ruffled my hair. Caron had set heart stones in the ring of hollow spaces. She'd put small ones across from small ones and bigger ones balanced against bigger ones. A huge stone lay at the top of the circle, with nothing even close in size to put at the bottom. I'd never seen one so perfectly round or a red so deep it was almost black.

"Governor Barth's?" I asked.

Caron nodded and turned back to the altar. "What can you tell me about this arrangement, Cade? All I know is what I've learned from books, and that says it's correct, but I'm not sure."

It wasn't. It was hard to describe what I felt around even a single heart stone. My blood flowed warmer. My skin tingled. My muscles yearned to get closer. Music hummed somewhere far off, calling me toward it.

But with a dozen stones on the altar, all those things bumped up against one another. My skin didn't tingle; it stung. The humming wasn't music; it was just noise. The pull on my muscles went every which way and was so strong, it hurt. I'd felt something like that in the blocked-up cellar, but this was worse. Whatever was happening must be stronger because we were in the world's center and the calendar change was closing in on us.

With Keled still dogging me, I circled the altar, eyeing each stone. "There are books about this?" I asked Caron. "What do they say?"

"They're manuscripts really, prophecies written by the wise ones who built this temple and the street shrines hundreds of years ago."

"I never heard of them."

"The miners' syndicate has them," Caron said. "They collect all the old lore about stones, hoping it will help them find new mines. But these manuscripts say a balanced circle of stones is the only thing that will keep disaster away. They say the earth will open and fire will consume us unless we create that balance."

I glanced at the pictures on the wall, then circled the altar again and stopped by the giant stone. "This one is throwing everything else off. It's beating them down and sort of absorbing them." Its pull was also beating on me so hard, I expected to see bruises.

Caron bit her lip and studied the altar. "But without that one, we have an empty space. How do we balance that?"

A teeny voice in my head said, *Maybe with the triangular stone?* I squashed it quiet. The governor's stone was bigger and had more power, which was surely a good thing. "Maybe move the others away from it?"

"But then they'd be out of the hollows," Keled said. "Is that the best you can do?"

"If you have another suggestion, go ahead and make it," I said.

He flushed and picked at a loose embroidery thread on his shirt.

"Are we sure the altar will still work with the temple in ruins like this?" I asked.

Shan's mouth pressed into a line. "We have to keep trying."

"It will," Caron said. "I'm certain, even if Shan isn't."

I decided I believed her. All the while I'd been in here, the feel of the stones had been growing. I needed to get out while I still could. "I have to go. I need to look for my mum."

Shan shot me a sympathetic look.

"I'll concentrate on balancing that big stone then," Caron said. "If the weather gets better, I'll know I have it right."

They all ignored me as I picked up my package and slipped out of the temple. That was fine by me. I had worries of my own. Caron sounded sure she could balance the stones, but what if she couldn't? When midnight came, I wanted Mum in our house with the triangular stone to protect her.

15. NEAR SCELD'S GATE

Dance while you can.—Mins, the musician god

When I pushed through our doorway, Roth lay on his pallet, staring at the ceiling. He turned his head toward me. I was as thrilled as if he'd stood up and danced a jig. This was my doing too.

"The last thing I remember is leaving work," he said. "What happened?"

"You've been sick. Are you hungry?"

"Not really. Help me to the privy though."

I did, and then brought him inside and lowered him to sit with his back propped against the wall. The short trip exhausted him. His eyes had purple shadows under them.

"I'll put the food and a cup of water where you can reach them," I said. "Then I have to go to work."

"All right." He slid down the wall to stretch out and close his eyes. "Be careful."

I laughed. "You really are getting better."

When I had things ready for him, I set out for our old neighborhood near Sceld's Gate. If Shan didn't have Mum, then maybe she was looking for me and Roth, and that meant she'd probably go to our old house. I thought of her blank, unresponsive face and swallowed down the pain in my throat. She'd have to remember us to look for us, but maybe even if she'd forgotten Roth and me, she'd go to Sceld's Gate, if only because it was familiar territory.

I headed north across the city. I hadn't gone three blocks before the ground rumbled and shook, knocking me to my knees. The bricks in a garden wall broke apart and fell all around me like dice shaken from a cup. I threw my hands over my head. A brick bounced off my shoulder, driving a cry out of me.

The rattling stopped, and I pulled myself to my feet, rubbed the pain away as best I could, and started walking faster. As I moved to wider and wider streets, I found myself in a stream of people heading out of town. Most of them were on foot, hurrying their kids along, faces wrinkled with worry, their belongings on their backs. But every little while, the clip clop of horses came from behind us, and a driver cracked his whip and shouted for us to get out of the way. We'd all crowd to the street's edge, and a carriage would whirl by.

"Filthy syndicate merchants." The old man walking next to me spat at a particularly big carriage, loaded with boxes and richly dressed people. "They take the good, and leave the bad to us. I hope one of those cracks opens up across the road and they drive right in."

I thought about Keled, who'd left home to help Jem, and though it pained me, I said, "Some of them aren't so bad."

The old man glared at me and sped up, leaving me behind.

By then, I was in Warriors Way, one of the main roads running from the old temple to a city gate. I was slow because I was looking down every lane we passed, hoping for a glimpse of Mum and getting more and more worried. From what I'd seen the day before, she might not be able to look after herself very well.

I stopped at a shrine. *I'm a Finder, I prayed. Help me find what matters to me.*

Along with other offerings, a heart stone was fused into the stone shelf, though it had no power any more, because that would all have gone back to the gods long ago. I thought about Mum trying to leave a stone in the Long Street shrine. Would I have the strength to leave a heart stone? The one under the table in my house, for instance? Not worth worrying about, I decided, since I didn't have it here. I left one of the pennies Shan had paid me and touched Ras the Trickster to show I was sorry about wanting to knock his teeth out. The last thing I needed was to have the gods angry with me. They were what they were, and you couldn't expect to understand why they did things.

Where Warriors Way crossed the Outer Circle, I came to the old north gate, Sceld's Gate, beyond which lay our old neighborhood. I'd seen fire over the housetops, and now I stopped to look at the god's eye burning in the wide dish atop the gate. The flame bloomed long and wide, at least three times its normal size. An image from the temple flared into my head: a wall of fire closing in on sick and scared people. My heart tripped. I plunged through the tunnel below the gate, where the already steamy air felt even hotter.

Beyond the gate, I went to our old house first. I slid my fingers over the three notches I'd cut in the windowsill when I was four and took Dad's big knife and went around seeing what it would cut. He was usually easy-going, but not that day. My backside still hurt when I remembered it. Mum's flowers were sending up green shoots next to the doorstep. I wanted to live here again so hard that I almost couldn't believe I didn't. It felt wrong to have to knock.

The door opened, and a man leaned against the frame. Above his curly beard, his face was flushed and his eyes dull. "What?" he growled.

I looked past his shoulder, but none of the furniture looked familiar. The landlord must have sold what we had. I felt like I'd lost something I treasured. "I'm looking for a woman named Mareth who used to live in this house. Have you seen her?"

"Never heard of her." He slammed the door.

I went next door, raised my hand to knock, and stopped. The neighbor would know me. What if they called the Watch because they thought I might be a Finder? I drew a deep breath. With midnight coming, it was too late to worry about myself. I knocked, but no one answered. Now what? All I could do was keep looking.

In Twisted Knee Lane, I was surprised to see a piper playing the traditional New Year music for a couple spinning in the dance that always made me sick when I tried it. Two women with mugs of ale sat watching them. One vaguely familiar woman had unbuttoned her gown at the throat, and a pus filled blister showed. I backed a step away. When I asked about Mum, the sick woman frowned.

"Her? She turned out to be a Finder. It's a wonder she didn't rob and murder us all."

I decided she had pus in her brain too. "A Finder wouldn't hurt you," I said, "though one might rob you if you had a heart stone. Do you?"

"Of course not." The sick woman's frown deepened.

"Some of the Crows have been around asking about her too," the other woman said. "The miner who owns her says she's run away, so the Crows are looking to see if she's come home."

My stomach flipped over. "Nobody owns her," I said and turned to question the piper who'd just finished playing.

"I saw a beggar woman this morning," he said. "Would that be her? At least I think she was a beggar. She was thin and looked like she'd been living hard."

"Where?" I asked.

The piper shrugged. "I can't remember exactly."

I knotted my hands into fists so I wouldn't grab him and shake a better answer out of his mouth. I'd turned away when two Watchmen came around the corner.

"All of you go home," one of the Watchmen told the piper, the dancers, and the watching women. "Governor Barth's forbidden crowds to gather."

"We're not a crowd," one of the women said. "It's New Year's Eve, you sour-faced dogs."

The Watchman took her arm and hauled her up from her bench. "Inside. Now."

I hurried around a corner. I kept an eye out but didn't see any more Watchmen as I roamed up one lane and down another, questioning the few people I met, my worry growing. No one but the piper had seen anyone out of place. What to do? Maybe our old neighbors had been chased home by the Watch.

I turned back into our street, then jammed to a halt. Two Crows were just stopping outside our house, but what really made my heart pound was that one of them was Wilder. I was backing up so fast my feet skidded when a woman stepped out of a doorway at the far end of the street. She was bone thin, but her head was down and she stood in shadow, so I couldn't be sure it was Mum.

I rocked back and forth.

Wilder knocked at our old house. When the door opened and the same sick man appeared, Wilder and the other Crow edged away, spooked by the fever. Wilder said something I couldn't hear, and all at once, I realized the man was pointing to me. Wilder turned to look in my direction.

"You!" He bolted toward me. The other Crow looked startled but ran after him. I whirled and tore into the maze of tiny streets, veering left, then right, their footsteps pounding behind me. I glanced over my shoulder to see them at a corner looking for which way I'd gone. I slid sideways between two buildings as the other Crow shouted, "There!" I wriggled along the knife-thin passage. In the next street, I doubled back, then cut through a yard. Years of hide-and-seek and tag had taught my feet which way to run in Sceld's Gate.

Chest heaving, I ducked into a doorway and looked back. Wilder was nowhere in sight. I waited. Still no sign of him. I couldn't wait any more. I needed to go back and see if that woman was really Mum. I trotted to the next lane and took it.

Fifty yards ahead, Wilder and the other Crow ran out of a side street. "There!" Wilder said, waving the other Crow on.

I spun to find a huge carriage maneuvering around the corner. I raced toward it. At the sight of me rushing it, the horse's eyes widened, and it reared in its traces, hooves flailing within a foot of my face. The driver cursed and yanked on the reins. I flung my arm up and turned back, but there was nowhere to go. Wilder slowed and flashed his teeth in a triumphant smile. He had me.

A bang like a lightning strike shattered the air. The ground trembled so hard that I stumbled and fell to one knee in the dirt. A crack opened across the lane between me and Wilder, yawning wide enough that houses on either side tipped crazily into the gap. One of them slid in with a crash loud enough to make my ears ring. Dirt boiled up. I scrambled away, coughing.

Wilder teetered on the edge, flapping his arms like he was trying to fly. At the last instant, the other Crow ran up, grabbed the back of his collar, and held on to him. Wilder sat down hard, chest heaving.

We stared at one another across the crack. Then, behind them, a thin figure edged out into the lane.

Mum.

Our eyes met, and her face lit up. It was like she'd been half asleep before and now she'd woken up. Her mouth formed my name. She was so close! But Wilder and a broken world lay between us. How was I ever going to get to her?

Wilder staggered to his feet. "Go around," he shouted at the other Crow. "There has to be somewhere we can get across."

Mum shrank back into the side street, but Wilder bolted into it too. I ran to the edge of the crack, but I couldn't fly across it any more than Wilder could. Think! Though Wilder was looking for Mum, he didn't know her. But he did know me. Every muscle in my body strained toward Mum, but there was only one way for me to go—away from her.

"You want to find out where I live?" I shouted, trying to make it sound like a taunt. "You never will unless you know the neighborhood where my dad grew up."

If Mum and Wilder both heard that, only one of them would know where to go.

I pivoted toward the corner, then made myself slow so I wouldn't scare the trembling horse any further.

"Keep off." The driver shooed me away with his whip, then tugged on the reins. "Come on," he coaxed the horse in a much nicer voice. "Back up now."

I flattened myself against a building, and tried to scrape between it and the wagon.

The horse reared again.

"Fool!" The driver flicked his whip and a line of fire burned across my shoulder.

I pushed harder and popped free. Then I took off like a jackrabbit. Ahead of me, Sceld's Gate and its god's eye straddled the street. I'd seen it only a couple of hours earlier and now it blazed higher and wider than I could have imagined. Heat washed over me twenty yards away. The big houses near it were made of stone and roofed with clay tiles, but smoke rose from the garden of the house on the left, and one of its second-floor shutters was burning. Behind the garden wall, men shouted for water.

I slowed, but the thought of Wilder made me speed up again. Maybe he'd think no one with any sense would run through that furnace and decide I'd gone a different way. I pelted along the gate's brick passage. The air was so hot, it was like being in an oven. The skin on my face seared. I could hardly breathe. I stumbled. How long was this tunnel?

Gasping for air, I tore out the other side. In a lane across the way, a wood shingle roof smoldered where sparks fell. One bit the back of my neck, and a tiny black hole glowed on my sleeve. I slapped it out and ran, with sweat stinging my eyes.

At last, I was far enough away to feel safe, from Wilder at least. I slowed and went on, breathing cooler air and fingering a place on my face that felt blistered. I had to go a long way around because I kept finding cracks. The corpse cart rumbled along one street. I turned a different way.

Finally, I headed into our street. Granny sat on her stool, leaning back against the wall with her eyes closed. I stopped.

"Granny?"

She blinked.

"You're not sick again, are you?" She shouldn't be, not with the triangular stone still under our table.

"Just sleepy," she said.

"Want me to help you inside to lie down?"

She shook her head. "Out here, at least I'm sure the roof won't fall on me."

I started to move on, but she caught my fingers in her spotted hand. "There's a woman looking for you, Cade."

I tripped and caught myself. "Who?" Had Mum beaten me across town?

"I don't know. I've never seen her before." Granny shifted on the stool. "I told her I didn't know you. I don't like strangers snooping around like that."

I smothered a groan. "What did she look like?"

Granny pursed her lips. "Brown hair. In her forties."

That could be a lot of women, but who else besides Mum would come around asking for me? I hoped it was Mum because, from what I'd just seen, the city was in a bad way, which meant Caron hadn't yet found out how to balance the stones in the temple. I wanted Mum in our house. "Where did she go?"

Granny pointed across the street to a side lane.

"If she comes again, tell her where we live," I said. "She's family."

"I didn't know you and Roth had any other family. Good." The hair on Granny's chin quivered silver in the sunlight. "Roth needs someone to look after him."

She surprised a laugh out of me. "You're right. He does. So send her to our house." The knot in my stomach loosened. If I waited, Mum would surely come, so at least she'd be safe—assuming she made it past Crows, cracking earth, and fire, and that she got here before midnight. I opened our door.

Roth was on his feet buttoning his shirt. Even in the time I'd been gone, he'd gained strength. He looked up. "Done with work already?"

I flapped my mouth, remembering I'd told him I was working today. "We quit early on account of it being New Year's Eve. You look great!" I came all the way in, picked up the plate of bread and cheese I'd left next to his pallet, and thumped it onto the table.

Something hard clattered to the floor. We both looked down at the heart stone gleaming on the scarred wood.

16. REVELATIONS

Certainty is for fools.—Myst, the shapeshifter god

I snatched up the triangular stone and cradled it against my chest, like that would mean Roth hadn't seen it. It lay warm in my hand. My whole body yearned toward it.

He licked his lips. "Where did you get that?"

The stone filled my head so full, I could hardly answer. "I found it. I'm a Finder."

"But it's the stone you gave Mum the night she vanished. So where did you get it? And when have you been anywhere near heart stones?" Roth's voice rose on each word. He grabbed for the stone. I tried to hang on, but he slapped it out of my grip, so it bounced away into a corner.

Despite the sting of his slap and how desperately I was scrambling for an explanation, I still felt empty when I lost touch with the stone.

Roth gripped the front of my shirt and pulled me onto my tiptoes. Oh yes. His strength was back. "Don't stand there thinking up lies! Where did you get that stone?"

All I could think of was the truth, so I told it to him—Shan, the altar in the temple, taking heart stones, saving the city. It came out jumbled because there was so much of it, really an amazing amount for five days of sneaking around.

Roth didn't even wait for me to finish. "You've been stealing." His voice was flat, like he better not let out what he was feeling. "Sneaking into rich people's houses, miners' houses, and stealing heart stones."

"Not really stealing," I said quickly. "Shan says the heart stones don't belong to the people who have them. They belong to the temple."

"Shan's a thief and is teaching you to be one too. When I have time, I'm going to break you into little pieces, but for now, get your things. We're leaving."

"Wait, Roth—"

He jabbed a shaky finger into my face. "Don't try to tell me you wanted that stone so you could save the city. Stones twist Finders. I've seen it, and so have you, so don't try to fool me, and even more, don't try to fool yourself. You kept it."

"I kept it for you."

"Are you sure?" Roth was breathing hard.

"Yes!"

He scanned my face like he was reading one of his books. "I'm not certain I believe you, but thank you. Now get your stuff."

"Wait!" I raised my voice. "I have to tell you about Mum. I saw her yesterday. I got her loose from the miner who had her, but we got separated. But then I saw her again a while ago, and she should be on her way here."

For a moment, silence filled the room. Roth had been reaching for his carry bag, but now he let his hand drop. "You found Mum?"

I told him what had happened at Malel's house and what I'd seen this morning, though I left out the stuff about Wilder. No point in stirring things up.

Just as I finished, someone knocked on the door. When I opened it, Granny hovered on the doorstep. "The woman who was looking for you came back," she said.

My heart jumped. Roth took a step toward the door.

Granny beckoned, and Shan and Caron came into view. Granny tipped her hand toward Caron and looked hopeful. "Here she is."

Roth bit back the start of a curse and ran his hand through his hair like he was going to tear it out.

I slumped onto my stool. Mum was still out there in the middle of disaster.

"This is Caron." Shan frowned at Roth, who glared back.

"You related to the boys?" Granny beamed at Caron.

"No," Caron said, "just a friend. Can I impose on you for a cup of water while the young people talk?" She slid Granny's hand into the crook of her elbow and turned her away from us.

Granny looked over her shoulder, eyeing Shan and then Roth, who were facing off like two dogs with one bone. "Maybe Cade should come with us?"

"It's Cade I need to talk to," Shan said.

Caron tugged on Granny's arm, and she tottered off.

Shan came inside and closed the door.

"Why don't you come in?" Roth said. "Help yourself to what's mine, and do whatever you want with it."

69

Well, that was a change. He had no trouble talking to Shan at all, even though she was a girl. Maybe it helped that Shan wasn't smiling.

She frowned at his tone, then swept a look around the room, her eyes sliding right over the heart stone hiding in the dust in the corner. If I ever needed proof that she had no feel for the stones, that was it. "I need to talk to Cade about the work he's doing for me, and it's rather private. Perhaps we could go into the other room?" She took a step toward the back door.

"There is no other room, princess. This is it." Roth kicked his pallet into a heap and shoved the other stool toward Shan. "And you and Cade have talked privately for the last time."

"I have some say in this, you know," I said.

"No, you don't," Roth said.

She glanced at me. "You told him?"

"He found...out." I'd almost said he found the triangular stone and barely remembered in time that Shan didn't know I'd kept it.

Shan sat, then rose and closed the shutters. She turned to look down her nose at Roth, though she had to tilt her head back to do it. "I take it you don't approve?"

"Approve of stealing? Stealing heart stones no less? No. What did you think you were doing, dragging Cade into your schemes? How could you put him in that kind of danger? He's a kid cursed with a skill that causes more trouble than you can imagine."

"Don't talk about me like that," I said. "Some people say Finding's a gift, not a curse. And there'd be a lot more trouble tonight if I weren't a Finder." Actually, it was hard to imagine more trouble than was outside our door right now. Still, Shan and Caron would fix it because of the help I'd given them, and Roth should admit that.

"Why are you here?" he asked Shan. "I thought you were done using him."

Shan turned from Roth to me. "Caron can't arrange the stones correctly."

I couldn't breathe. If Caron couldn't get the stones right, everything we'd done had been for nothing. Everyone in the city was doomed. Mum was out there. Jem sat in the Crow's Hole. The moment Shan left our house and its stone, she'd be in trouble too.

"Caron tried everything," Shan went on. "She hopes it's just that Governor Barth's stone is too big, and something smaller would work better. You and I need to go back to Malel's house to see if the stone is there."

"He's not going," Roth said.

My gaze flicked to the corner. Maybe the triangular stone would work better than the governor's stone in the temple, and maybe it wouldn't, but I'd seen proof that it protected our house and kept Roth well. How could I give it to Shan now?

The nasty voice in my head said, *If rich folks are selfish for keeping stones, what does that make you?*

Roth's gaze went to the corner too, and I could almost see him remembering the stone. He opened his mouth, as if to tell Shan, then closed it and frowned at me. He was probably thinking about protecting me.

I thought about what Roth had asked me. Was I sure I'd been stealing heart stones because I wanted to help? Help who? Me and mine? Where was the border between people I should help and people I could let die? If I had a gift, like I'd just claimed, didn't I owe something back? Everything I'd seen in the last few days came flooding back to me: dying people, cracking earth, wild weather, the oversized fire in the gods' eyes. And Shan, Keled, Caron, and Jem, who could have taken stones back to wherever they lived and instead had taken them for the temple. I admired the people they were. What kind of person was I?

I gave a strangled laugh. "I'm sorry, Roth. I have to let her have it."

"Let me have what?" Shan said.

I started for the corner, but Roth put out a hand to stop me from touching. He picked up the stone, rubbed the dust on his trouser leg, and set it on the table.

We all stared at it. It sang softly, but I was the only one in the room who heard it. I had to admit I wanted it.

"Where did you get that?" Shan asked.

"I kept it when we were in the Malel house."

"You—" She was breathing hard. "How could you? I trusted you."

"I'm sorry. Roth was sick."

"Lots of people are sick!" Shan cried. "People at my house are sick! People all over the city. You'd have let them die. What is wrong with you?"

I felt like a louse on a flea on a rat.

"You found what you came for," Roth said. "Now take it and get out."

Shan ground her teeth. "I'd like to, but Caron says she needs Cade to help arrange the stones. He has to come."

"No," Roth said. "He's staying with me."

A tiny part of me wanted to do it, wanted to curl up and still be a little kid and let Roth take care of me. "What about Mum?" I said.

"What about everyone else? Shan needs me. If I hadn't kept the stone, Caron probably would have figured things out by now."

"I won't let you go," Roth said.

"Then you really will have to tie me up."

The muscles in Roth's jaw tightened. We looked at one another for a long moment, and then he turned away and swung a fist at the wall, pulling his punch only at the last instant. He shook his hand and sucked on a skinned knuckle. The wall had a new dent. "I'm going with you."

"You have to stay here and wait for Mum," I said. "She could still come."

He rocked from one foot to the other, face twisted in anguish that I didn't think came just from his bruised hand.

"I'll be fine," I said. "I'll have heart stones near me."

He gave a wordless cry. "Oh, that makes me feel so much better." He sank onto a stool and put his head in his hands. "If you take any chances, I swear I'll truss you like a turkey and tie you to the rafters."

"Don't worry," I said, though I knew I might as well ask him not to put his trousers on before he went to work.

"We need to go." Shan's bitter voice made me cringe. "We've wasted way too much time when we could have had that stone all along. Caron spent hours trying, and you have to get it right by midnight."

No pressure then.

I took a step toward the door, then back to Roth. "Maybe you should wait for Mum out front, like Granny's doing, just in case the house falls in."

Shan snorted. "You two are quite the pair." She yanked the door open. "Where's Caron?"

"Cade will get her," Roth said. "I want to talk to you."

"He wants to tell you not to bruise me." I slid past Shan into the lane and closed the door on them. I didn't want to look at Shan's betrayed face or Roth's worried one.

No one was outside Granny's, and no voices came through the open window, but when I knocked, Caron answered. There was no sign of Granny.

I went in, closed the door, and spoke low. "Are you ready? We have the extra stone. Don't ask," I said when she opened her mouth. "I don't want to explain again."

She pursed her lips and half lowered her eyelids. She'd been Shan's governess, so she probably recognized guilt when she saw it. "Wait a moment so I can say goodbye to Granny. She's in the privy."

I paced to the back door and had pivoted to pace to the front one when Crows passed Granny's window. My heart flew into my throat. I ran to look out.

The Crows stopped by our door. There were three of them and an officer and a boy. The officer was Captain Menard from Syndicate House. The boy was Jem the Finder.

17. THE MARKERS

Wisdom is found only if you seek it.—Lerned, the wise god

"Here?" Captain Menard asked.

"Yes," Jem said.

Taking Jem's arm to pull him aside, Menard nodded to his Crow underlings. They drew their swords, and the one in front kicked our door open. They rushed inside. Shan and Roth both yelled.

I tried to run for Granny's door, but Caron caught both my arms and blocked my way so I'd have to trample her to get there.

Granny hobbled in from the privy. "What's the matter?"

"Crows at my house," I gasped.

"Don't let him out," Caron said.

"Captain, what's the meaning of this?" Shan's voice came from outside. I heard her clearly because all the neighbors had gone quiet. Either they'd left town, or they didn't want the Crows to so much as blink in their direction.

"Miss Shandral?" Menard said.

"Shan!" Jem said. "I'm sorry! I didn't know you were here."

What was happening? I stopped struggling with Caron and craned my neck to see out the window. My heart tripped. One of the Crows clutched the triangular stone, while the other two held on to Roth. Blood trickled from a cut near his eye, but he was steady on his feet. He glanced my way and gave a tiny shake of his head. Shan faced Captain Menard with her hands on her hips.

"Beg pardon, Miss Shandral," the captain said. "We're looking for whoever's stealing heart stones, including your father's. According to the foreman he worked for, the boy who lives here was in a house when it was robbed, and Jem said this house held a stone."

Miss Shandral? Her father's stone? Tricky gods. Shan was Governor Barth's daughter. The edges of the world darkened. When my vision cleared, Roth was glaring at her, and even Jem was goggle-eyed, but one look at Caron told me she'd known. Of course she had. Liars, both of them.

"Jem was mistaken, Captain," Shan said coolly. "Father's stone isn't here."

"But this one was, sir." The Crow gave the triangular stone to the captain.

Menard turned it over, then raised his gaze to Roth. "Where did you get this?"

"It's mine." Shan extended her hand. "Give it to me, please."

The captain hesitated, then closed his fingers around the stone. "A lot of people at your father's house are down with fever, Miss, including my wife. The household needs a stone, and maybe this one would do." He jerked his head at the Crows. "Bring him along. We'll let Governor Barth sort this out."

"It's mine." Shan's voice rose.

"I can't give it to you on my own authority," the captain said. "Surely you can see that, Miss."

The Crows were already moving away with Roth. I lunged, but Caron and Granny both flung themselves between me and the door.

"Think, Cade," Caron said. "They're Guards. They have swords."

"They have Roth," I cried.

"Let Shan look out for him. Trust her," Caron said.

"That liar?"

"What's happening?" Granny sounded bewildered, but she plastered herself across the door.

I shoved Caron aside, then flailed my arms, looking for a place to grab Granny without breaking her.

"Cade, we need to get the stones and go to the temple," Caron said. "That's what's important now. With the stone you had gone, we have to balance the governor's, and that's going to be hard. Please! We'll help your brother and Shan once the city is safe."

I picked Granny up by the waist and set her aside. The street was empty, and when I ran to the corner where the house had nearly fallen in, that street was empty too. Oh gods. Roth was gone, along with the triangular stone.

Caron ran up behind me, breathing hard. "Do you want Granny to die? Do you want everyone in the city to burn or be swallowed by the earth or drop dead of fever?"

Mum. Roth. Everyone.

A sudden idea made hope flash through me. "All right. We'll go to Syndicate House too. We'll spring Roth at the same time we get the stones from the cellar."

"The stones aren't at Syndicate House," Caron said. "We moved them after Shan took the governor's stone because the feel of ours would be unmasked."

So I could leave Roth in the hands of the Crows, or I could leave everyone in the city, including Mum, to whatever fate had in store for them at midnight. Any choice I made led to grief and guilt. A piece of broken table lay in the mud of the street. I picked it up and threw it at the shattered wall of the house it had spilled out of. It landed with a smack, knocking loose another chunk of wall. "Where are they?"

Caron closed her eyes, and her shoulders dropped in relief. "They're at Keled's. Come." She set off in the other direction. I took a last look down the street where Roth had gone, then went after her.

#

"What do you mean you don't know where Keled lives?" I said. "You and Shan let him take all the heart stones, and you're not sure where they wound up?"

Caron held a stray lock of hair back against the shrieking wind. "Shan knows which place is his. All I know is that he lives here in the Markers. We'll just have to ask around."

We were in the oldest part of Cor, not far from the temple. The skinny, round buildings took their name from the grave markers they resembled, and they weren't just old. They were falling-down ancient. Armies of rats made war on the people in them, and these people were all really poor, or they wouldn't live there. When I was little, Mum forbade me to play here, so I hardly ever did. And when Roth and I needed a new place to live, he refused to even look in the Markers. It had never occurred to me that a jeweler like Keled might live in these tenements.

"We don't have to ask," I said. "I can find it." I scanned the tipsy, three-story buildings. They all looked alike, but if a dozen heart stones, including Governor Barth's giant one, were there, I should be able to pick out where they hid. Faint waves of their power washed over me even now. I circled a pile of rotting garbage and trotted into the shadowy canyon between two buildings. "No wonder Shan talked so easily about 'owning' Finders. She's the daughter of Governor Barth, the head of the miners' syndicate. She's probably just like him."

"You know she's not," Caron said. "She's fought being like him since she was ten. If anything, stealing stones he was hoarding made it more satisfying for her."

"How nice she could enjoy herself."

"I suppose you never lied about what you are and weren't enjoying yourself at all," Caron said, sounding a whole lot like Mum on the verge of losing her temper. "And Shan took the stone protecting her home."

"Only when she had no other choice," I said.

"And why was it that she had no choice? Captain Menard found a stone in your house. So what does that tell me?"

I hunched my shoulders against an argument that was too much for me and stomped down the space between the houses. Being mad at Shan helped me shove away my fears for Roth and Mum.

The buildings curved away to right and left, forming new alleys. The call of the heart stones pulled me left. A rat skittered up the side of a building and vanished into a hole in the wall. At the next curved corner, the stones' warring energies burst over me. I jogged to a Marker leaning like a two-legged sheep and jangling with the powers of a bunch of heart stones. Despite the way it made me cringe, I wanted in there, and I wanted in now.

"Which floor?" Caron asked.

I paused outside the ground floor door, then tipped my head back and looked up. Rickety stairs wound around the outside of the oversized shack. I giant-stepped over the missing bottom stair and started up. A railing would have been nice. The stairs tilted outward, threatening to slide me and Caron off the edge. I passed the second floor and stopped outside the top door.

Caron knocked. The door clicked and cracked open, and Keled peered out.

"You found him. Good." He opened the door all the way, let us in, and locked it behind us, leaving the key in the door.

My whole body stung with the clashing music of the stones. It flooded the room so completely I couldn't tell exactly where it came from. Except for the feel of a fortune in heart stones, the place wasn't much. Light came only from two small windows high up under the ceiling. Through an open door, I glimpsed two pallets and one of Keled's silk shirts on a hook. The floor slanted enough that the blankets had slid off the pallets and the shirt leaned like it wanted to see what we were doing. This wasn't what I expected from Keled at all.

"What's the matter? Did you think I ate off gold dishes?" Keled sneered at me, like I'd said something, which I hadn't.

"Where are the stones?" Caron asked.

Still sneering, Keled went into the bedroom. A gray cat padded out of the shadows and rubbed against my leg. When I squatted to stroke it, it purred.

"That's Fog," Caron said. "He's Jem's, and he's usually standoffish." She cocked her head. "Maybe he likes Finders."

The animals at Master Joff's stable always took to me. Maybe that was because I was a Finder. That thought was somehow comforting. Animals loved you for what you were. Unlike a lot of people, they didn't care if you were old or ugly or poor. If they thought being a Finder was a good thing, it couldn't be so bad.

Keled came back with a box, set it on the table, and opened it. I pressed closer. A dozen heart stones were heaped in the box with the governor's stone on top. Under its drag, the rest of the stones felt like sharp needles. When I slid my sleeve over my hand and reached to nudge it aside, Keled jerked the box away, rattling the stones. I flinched. The cat jumped up on the table and nosed at the box.

"We need to be on our way to the temple," Keled said. "Where's Shan?"

I snorted. "At Syndicate House." When his eyes widened in horror, I took my chance to sneer. "You didn't know? You don't have to worry for her. She's the governor's daughter."

"What?" He looked at Caron, who grimaced but nodded. "She knows where we are." Keled's voice rose. "She knows where the stones are. What's she doing?"

"She's not doing anything," Caron said. "Governor's Guards caught her and took her home, but I know her as if she were my own daughter. Trust her."

"This is hopeless." Keled sank onto a stool. "The Guard is after us, and you can't balance the stones, which means Half-pint here certainly can't."

"Let me see." I reached for the box again, and this time he was so beat down he let me pull it out from under his hand. The cat sat to watch as I took the stones out one by one, careful not to let them touch my skin. They shone every shade of red and every shape, and even through my shirt, they pulsed with life against my hand. The feel of them jolted through my body, making my heart race and my brain drum against the inside of my skull. A dozen different kinds of music banged together. The best you could say for that was it kept me from sinking into myself in a fit of stone sickness. Gritting my teeth, I spread the stones out in a circle, then moved them around. Every time I picked the governor's stone up, the other stones sounded less grating. Every time I put it down, the song of the others swirled toward it and faded into a tangled mess.

"You can't balance them, can you?" Keled said.

"Shut up," I said.

"Maybe it will be better in the temple," Caron said.

"The governor's stone is the problem," I said. "It gobbles up all the others." I let go of the giant stone, and it rolled across the table, leaving a scarlet trail in the dim light. The cat's head turned to watch as I caught it.

"If only you and Shan had found that other stone." Keled rubbed his forehead. "Can't you get it on your own?"

I flicked a look at Caron, who gave me an equally quick glance.

"What is it?" Keled sat up straight, looking from me to Caron with narrowed eyes.

I cleared my throat. "We did find it. Only I kept it."

"You what?" Keled stood so quickly that the stool tipped over and rolled to the low end of the room. The cat jumped off the table and fled into the bedroom.

"I didn't mean to, but my brother was sick."

Keled's fists closed and opened. Then he jumbled the rest of the stones into their box. "So you and Shan are both liars, and we've failed to save the city. Wonderful. At least I can save Jem. Give me that." He reached to take the governor's stone from me.

I backed away. "What do you mean?"

"I'm taking them all to Syndicate House and trading them for Jem." He snatched at my hand.

"No!" I scrambled away. "Saving Jem won't be enough. The whole city is in trouble, maybe the whole world." And when I argued that to

Keled, I finally convinced myself it was true. Saving Jem wouldn't be enough. Saving Roth and Mum wouldn't either.

"Haven't you been listening? We can't save the whole world." He lunged around the table and came after me. In the small room, he didn't have a long way to come. I twisted away, holding the stone as far out of his reach as I could.

"Stop!" Caron cried. "Cade and I have to go to the temple. We have to."

"Rich folks are keeping their stones to save just the ones they care about too," I said to Keled. "You want to be like that?"

The buzzing in my body got stronger, and only when I heard the rumble did I realize it wasn't the feel of the stones. Somewhere nearby, the ground was splitting open, and shaking the whole shambling building like it meant to knock it to splinters. The box of stones fell off the table, spilling some of them out to slide away. Caron fell to her hands and knees, then crept to sweep them up.

Keled pinned my shoulder to the wall and reached. I swung Governor Barth's stone around and whacked him on the head. When he staggered, let go of me, and dropped to his knees, I ran for the door.

Caron came after me, clutching the box of stones. I snatched the key from the lock. We erupted onto the stairway, and I slammed and locked the door.

As soon as we were out the door, I saw a jagged crack opening between Keled's building and the next one. The stairs shook. Caron fled down them, but I hesitated, then shoved the key under Keled's door before I clattered after her. I was within two yards of the ground when the steps tore away from the building and collapsed into a pile of broken wood, dumping me into a stunned heap. Caron pulled me to my feet, and we ran away from the crack, both looking over our shoulders. Keled's building swayed but didn't fall, and then the ground steadied.

My heart still galloped around in my chest, trying to catch up to the news we were safe.

Caron's hand trembled on my arm. She drew a long breath, tightened her hold on the box of stones, and nodded toward where the globes of the temple spire slanted over the surrounding roofs. "Let's go."

I wanted to. The heart stones she carried pulled at me like a string tugging on kid's wheeled ducky.

"You go." I shoved the governor's stone into my pocket. "I'll meet you there." I trotted away.

"I need that," she cried. "Where are you going?"

"To Syndicate House," I called back. "Keled had the right idea. I'm going to trade it."

"For your brother?"

I pushed the shiny idea away. "For the triangular stone." I broke into a run and headed for the governor's.

18. SYNDICATE HOUSE

Choose old or choose bold.—Ras, the trickster god

I leaned into the wind and blinked to scrape grit off my eyeballs. Could those red lights in the sky be gods' eyes? I shouldn't have been able to see any of them from here, much less three, but they bloomed like fat red flowers. Houses must be burning too, and from the smell, what I'd thought were clouds was really smoke. At every corner, the gale swirled into whirlwinds loaded with dirt and trash. I flung away a broken vine caught on my leg, and it landed on a huddled shape that turned into a body when I looked more closely. I ran on, trying not to think about Mum, loose and confused in the streets. The day was fading into dark. Midnight was coming.

I tore out onto the Inner Circle but jammed to a halt at the sight of the mob surging around Syndicate House. Beyond the gates, the yard was full of Crows.

"Let us in!" a man shouted, a smith by the look of his arms.

"The miners must have heart stones," cried a woman, whose hair was whipped into her face by the wind. "The fire's driving us out of our homes. Governor Barth has to take us in."

The crowd swelled forward like a wave on a lake. The gates flexed but held.

"We don't have any heart stones here," lied a lying liar Crow. "Try the old temple. That's a holy place, isn't it?"

"No." I plunged into the crowd, waving my arms. "That place is a ruin." I didn't want them here, but I didn't want them at the temple either.

The crowd was so big and noisy that hardly anyone heard me, but the ones close by turned to see who I was.

"The temple might shield us," said a fever-flushed man right in front of me.

"No," I cried. "It's dangerous. The roof is falling in."

The feverish man had taken a step away, but now he turned back to Syndicate House. A handful of people broke off to go to the temple, but the rest pushed toward the gate again. Tricky gods. I shouldn't have stopped them leaving. Now what?

I pushed back the way I'd come and ran along the street, scanning its edge. There! That was the alcove in the garden wall, and there was the sewer grid.

I crouched, pulled the grid off the drain, and lowered myself into the sewer. To my shock, water rose all the way to my waist. I nearly stumbled from surprise and was glad I didn't because the water reeked of garbage and privies. From inside the drain, I wasn't tall enough to reach the grid and put it back, but I doubted if anyone else would see crawling into an open drain as a good idea. I slogged through the water. Something slimy washed up against me and swept past. I didn't look because I didn't want to know what it was. With night pressing down, the only light through the grids to the street came from the lanterns and torches carried by the mob.

The ground shook, knocking me off my feet. Sewer water flooded my mouth. I bobbed up, retching, and then ran, the governor's heart stone quivering in my pocket. I hadn't gone more than five yards before my hand slapped empty space. This had to be the right corner. I rounded it and kept running, water churning around me. Ahead, the darkness lightened. Weak with relief, I slipped through the opening and was once again in the flooded cellar with its collapsed and rotting wooden shelves. I waded across to the steps as fast as my shaking legs would take me.

A roar boomed from behind me, followed by the crash and splash of stones hitting water. A wave surged across the storeroom, shoving me into the steps. I looked back to see rubble blocking the opening to the drain. Tricky gods. The sewer had fallen in. How was I going to escape? Fear grabbed my throat, sending me scrambling for another way out.

There had to be a door somewhere. Shan had said the cellar was "blocked up," but surely that didn't mean closed by bricks or stones. They'd just abandoned it because it flooded, so there'd be maybe a few boards. I could deal with boards.

Frantically, I scanned the storeroom walls but they looked solid, so I went into the higher room, where at least so far, the water was only halfway up my shins. The table and shelves still stood against the wall, but Keled must have taken his tools and other stuff when he took the heart stones. His glass-making furnace glowed with a banked fire, the source of the room's dim light, but water lapped near the furnace door, so there wouldn't be light for long. The thought of being in the dark in here made more sweat sprout in my armpits. I made a hasty circuit of the room. No door. But there had to be one. The governor's servants hadn't come in and out of here through the sewer.

My heart thudded, reminding me of time slipping away toward midnight.

I went back down to the storeroom and searched for a door around its edge with water closing in on my chest. I had a vision of floating trapped against the ceiling with water rising. The room went fuzzy. I would drown here. No one would ever find me. Roth and Mum would die too, one way or another.

That thought was like a slap. Roth and Mum die? Stink on that. Not if I could help it.

I sloshed back to the foot of the stairs, started up, and stopped. Lower down like this, I could see under the table, and there it was—the bottom half of a door.

I hastened across the room, but when I tried to shove the table out of the way, the thing turned out to be heavy as a horse. The shelves wobbled though, and I realized they'd just been set on the table. I flung my shoulder against them, cringing at the smart of the whip mark the wagon driver had left there. The shelves slid off with a splash loud enough to spook a deaf man.

I heaved at the table. The water had risen far enough to lighten it now, and I managed to slide it away from the wall. I pulled the door open to face three boards nailed across the doorway, too close together for me to squirm between them. There was plenty of room for the water though, and it rushed into the stairwell and rose up the steps. I rammed the boards with the other shoulder, but they'd been solidly nailed. I needed something hard to bash one of them in with. Would it have hurt Keled to leave me a hammer? I hadn't come this far to be stopped by a hunk of wood.

The governor's stone sent a painful spurt of power up my right side. *Ha! Good idea.* I pulled the hulking thing out and used it to smash the middle board. I hunched, stepped through, and groped my way up the dark stairwell and out of the water—for now anyway. One floor, a second one, a third. Doors opened off each landing, hiding bins of vegetables, barrels of wine, jars of oil. I kept climbing.

As I went, my brain careened around, looking for the best way to trade Governor Barth's stone for the triangular one. I concluded that "best" was another way of saying "without telling Governor Barth."

I turned a corner. The steps rose to one more door and went no further. When I cracked the door open, the smell of roasting meat shot up my nose. My stomach growled, though I managed not to moan. I was near the kitchen then. Across the landing, a barred door probably led to the yard where supplies would be brought in by people like me and Elgar. Worried voices came from my right where I glimpsed the edge of a table with pots and pans hanging from hooks over it.

"What if that mob breaks in?" The girl's voice was rough, and she gave a loud sniffle.

"The Governor's Guard will keep them out," a man answered. "Nearly all of them are out in the front yard."

"Will they keep the fire out too?" asked a woman who sounded older and a whole lot less weepy.

I slid out onto the landing and darted left, away from the voices and into a hallway with the now familiar look of servant quarters. There, I closed my eyes and tried to feel the triangular stone but sensed only the powerful pull of the one in my pocket. My breath quickened. Surely the triangular stone was here. Governor Barth wouldn't trust it as much as the giant one I carried, but he'd see it as better than nothing.

I tiptoed toward the center of the house. The chances were the stone was in the heartroom, where its power would be strongest. As I went, I kept searching for the stone's feel and not finding it. I squeezed the governor's stone through my pocket, but it wouldn't shut up.

The servants' hallway ended at a screened opening, the way they usually did, but when I peeked around the screen, there was a crossing hallway rather than the heartroom I expected. The new hallway was wide and lined with tapestries, so I'd reached the end of servantland.

I crept out, and as I stood looking left and then right, the feel of the governor's stone soured and swirled up my spine. I stiffened, then lunged to lay my hands flat on the wall in front of me. Yes! I felt the warm pull of the triangular stone! The heartroom must be on the other side of this wall.

I ran along the hallway as silently as I could, passing closed doors and a stairway. At the corner, I made myself stop and leaned out to check for company.

Behind me somewhere, voices sounded.

"He took his time," Shan said. "Did he tell you to give me my heart stone?"

"No, Miss." Captain Menard sounded harassed.

"Why not?" Shan snapped. "It's mine, not his."

"You can ask him that, Miss," Menard said.

Truly, I understood his frazzled tone. Shan could wear on you sometimes.

They were coming down the stairs. I opened a random door and ducked into the room. It turned out to be a privy with a china pot under a carved seat, but it smelled just like the privy in my yard. Good to know some things are the same for rich and poor alike.

I left the door open a sliver and put my eye to the gap. The captain escorted Shan past, gripping her arm. As soon as they vanished around the corner, I slid out and followed. They went through a wide archway into what I figured was the heartroom.

From what they'd been saying, I also figured Governor Barth was in there, but I couldn't let that stop me. Midnight was closing in.

At the archway, I craned my neck to look in and then gritted my teeth at the prickling pain that immediately flickered over my skin. It was good pain because it meant the triangular stone was there, clashing with the stone I had in my pocket. I eyed a jeweled box on the central altar.

"Your daughter, sir," Menard said, and I tore my gaze away from the altar to where Shan, the captain, and Governor Barth were gathered at the room's other side.

Governor Barth sat straight-backed in a big chair, carved with the pickaxe symbol of the miners' syndicate. I'd seen him riding through the city, but never this close. Even sitting down, he was tall. His eyes were flat blue pebbles. One of his rings probably cost as much as Roth and I together would make in our lifetimes.

Shan shook off Menard's hand and marched right up to her father. She'd said she was afraid of him, but I'd never guess it from watching her. It wouldn't have surprised me if she spit in his eye. "So you're finally ready to hear me," she said.

"I find it's best to learn what you've been up to before I hear you, Shandral," Governor Barth said. "That way, it's easier to tell when you're lying." His mouth barely moved when he talked, like he resented having to spend the words.

Shan tossed her head and turned to Captain Menard, waiting respectfully to one side. "The captain stopped me in the street and arrested one of my friends. Tell him to let Roth go."

One eyebrow raised, Governor Barth turned to the captain too.

I crouched and ran to put the altar between us, then popped up long enough to grab the box. It was heavy as an anchor. I had to slide it rather than lift it, cringing all the time because its bottom scritched on the altar.

Shan's glance flicked toward me and away again. She moved so the captain and her father would be turned even more away from the altar if they wanted to look at her. "That stone is mine, Father." Her voice boomed, covering any sound I might make.

I sank down, cushioning the box's fall with my hands and one knee. *Ow, ow, ow.* When the blackness faded, I clawed at the clasp on the box. It didn't move. *It's locked, you fool. What did you expect?* Now what? Take the whole box and try to crack it open at the temple? I could barely lift it.

Governor Barth was speaking. "What did you learn about the prisoner, Captain? Is he a Finder?"

"He doesn't seem to be," Menard said, "but as you know, he did have a stone."

"So he's just a thief," Governor Barth said. "Very well. I'll try him later. He'll hang just as well after New Year."

Suddenly, there was no air in the room. I peered around the edge of the altar.

"Roth's not a thief," Shan said. "He's my friend."

"Unfortunately, being your friend is no guarantee he's not a thief." Governor Barth rose and walked toward her. For a moment, they faced one another. They had the same tilted nose and the same tight set to their jaws. "Where's my stone, Shandral? This one is small, and we need all the power we can gather. Where's mine?"

Roth, I urged her silently. *Get back to telling your creepy father to let Roth go.*

"Are you saying I had something to do with it going missing?" She pressed a hand to her chest and looked insulted. "This is my home. Why would I take our heart stone?"

"You'd take it to spite me. Caron probably egged you on. I should have exiled her instead of just dismissing her." Governor Barth stepped right into Shan, like he thought she'd back away. Had the man spent no time at all with his daughter? "People in this house have been sick, maybe dying. Did you want to hurt them as well as me?"

"You don't care about them," Shan said. "You only care about you."

"I'm not the one who hurt them," Governor Barth said. "Where's my stone?"

She lifted her chin and smiled.

Quick as a lizard's tongue, he shot out his hand, seized her wrist, and twisted.

Shan gave a single cry, then clamped her mouth shut.

I must have made a noise because Captain Menard turned his head and looked straight at me. I jumped to my feet, dumping the box with a noise like a horse kicking over an anvil. I danced around it and ran like my rear was on fire. Behind me, Shan gave a wordless cry, and the captain swore.

"Out of the way, Miss!" he said.

I tore back the way I'd come. Footsteps pounded out of the heartroom as I rounded the corner temporarily out of sight of whoever it was. Very temporarily. Should I duck into one of these rooms? With no other way out, I'd be a rat in a trap. Flee through the servant quarters and out that back door? I had to get Roth out of there, and I still needed the triangular stone. Where would they not expect me to go?

The stairway loomed. I bounded up it, three steps at a time, glimpsing the captain running past as I reached the landing. I pelted down the upstairs hallway, trying frantically to map the house in my head. There were doors only on my right. The solid wall on my left must be the upper part of the high-ceilinged heartroom. The captain and the governor would be out of there, looking for me, meaning now was my best chance to take the triangular stone.

The hallway turned and halfway down it was the stairway I needed. My back pressed to the wall, I sidestepped down it, breathing in little gasps. At the bottom of the stairs, I looked both ways. Not four yards away was an entry into what had to be the heartroom. I took a step toward it, and nearly ran into Governor Barth, spurting out of a side hallway. His chest was heaving, and his face was red from running, but when he saw me, his mouth curved.

"Captain!" he shouted. "He's here."

I pulled the huge stone from my pocket and flung it past him. Well, I flung it at him, but it went past him. I was glad to be rid of the oversized thing. It ate at my mind like a hungry wolf.

Governor Barth's eyes got huge, and he whirled to go after it, just as the captain galloped around the corner. They collided, and both went down. It was one of the best things I'd seen in a long time.

"Fool!" Governor Barth shouted. "Get him!"

By then, I was on my way into the heartroom. How was I going to run weighed down by that box? I'd have to just do it.

Shan straightened from where she'd been crouched behind the altar. When she saw me, she held up her hands. In one, she clutched her lockpicks. In the other was the triangular stone.

"This way," she said, running for the archway I'd gone out the first time.

I sped after her, but I could hear the captain huffing and puffing. Shan ducked into a side hallway, yanked open a door, and pulled me into what was probably a buttery where food and drink were brought from the kitchen and waited to be served in the heartroom. A pitcher of wine stood on a shelf, along with a meat pie and a tray of cinnamon cakes.

Shan opened a second door at the far end of the room and peered out. "We'll go out through the cellar," she said.

"We can't." Cinnamon cake crumbs sprayed out of my mouth and over Shan's back. "The sewer's collapsed."

She thought for a moment. "All right. There's another way. Come on."

She led me down one hall and into a second one.

"Look that way!" the captain shouted.

I jumped, but his voice came from the other side of the wall.

Another hallway cut in from our right. Shan put out her hand to stop me and leaned to speak in my ear. "Wait here." Before I could stop her, she put the triangular stone in my bare hand and hurried into the new hallway.

I stroked my thumb over the stone and listened to it sing. Maybe someone else could save the city. I could just stay here with the stone. Wouldn't that be easier?

With as much strength as it ever took me to do anything, I stuck the stone in my pocket and took my hand away.

I peeked around the corner to see what Shan was up to. The usual closed doors were on either side, but the hallway ended at a thick, heavy one.

Shan beat her fist against it. "Help!" she cried. "It's Shandral. Come out and help me!"

The door opened, and a Crow appeared, his sword half drawn.

I jerked back out of sight. A room with a Crow. Wonderful.

"There's someone here." Shan's voice trembled so hard, even I was half-convinced she was scared. "One of those people from outside got in," she said. "I saw him. He hid in there."

I leaned out to see her pointing a shaking finger at a door.

The Crow frowned. "That's not likely, Miss."

"Please look," she said. "Please."

He drew his sword and opened the door. Behind him, Shan lifted the heavy ring of keys from his belt, muffling its rattle with her other hand.

"You see?" the Crow said. "No one's here."

"Look in the chest." Shan elbowed him farther into the room, silently sorting through the keys. "He might be hiding in there."

He sighed and vanished into the room. Shan waved at me, urging me through the heavy door, which still stood open. I ran softly toward it. Through it, I glimpsed a bare stone floor and, almost too far to the side to see, metal bars.

Tricky gods. We were escaping into the Crows' Hole.

19. GIVING BACK THE GIFT

The world is made of the gods' music.—Mins, the musician god

I ducked through the doorway, with Shan right behind me, her skirt barely clearing the door before she locked it. We were in a narrow corridor with a stout door at the far end, and a stool and small table holding the Crow's dinner. Across from the table was a row of cells.

In the first cell, Roth and Jem jumped to their feet and rushed to the bars. A bruise was darkening on one side of Roth's face, but other than that, he looked all right, if I ignored the horrified look on his face. Apparently only one of us was glad to see the other.

"What are you doing here?" He gripped the bars hard enough to whiten his knuckles.

"Miss Shandral?" The Crow knocked on the door. "Open the door."

"Is the invader gone?" Shan called as she hurried to the door leading to the yard. She examined the keys. "Until he is, I feel so much safer in here."

"There is no invader." The Crow knocked harder. "Open the door."

I grinned at Roth. "I needed Mum's stone, so I came to get it. I figure I might as well rescue you along the way."

"Idiot!" he cried. "Why didn't you get away?"

"Shh." Shan unlocked the yard door, then came back to the cell. "I'm looking for the right key," she called to the Crow. "I'm going as fast as I can." She shuffled through the keys again and spoke more softly to Roth. "Has anyone ever told you how sweet it is that you try so hard to protect Cade?"

Sweet? Roth?

Roth's mouth fell open, and his face went pink. "I don't seem to be succeeding," he muttered.

"Where's Keled?" Jem asked.

"The temple, I hope." Shan glanced at me for the answer.

"He's at home," I said.

Shan frowned. "He let Caron go alone?"

"He had to take care of Jem's cat."

Shan shook her head, then chose a key and tried it in the lock. When it turned out to be the wrong one, she looked again.

A terrible thought occurred to me. "Wait." I put a hand on her arm. "We're not sure we can balance the stones in the temple, but your father's stone should keep this house safe. Leave Roth and Jem here."

Shan cocked her head, then nodded and stepped away from the hand Roth was reaching toward the keys.

"Give me that key." Roth shook the bars like he could tear them down. "If Cade goes, I'm going too."

"No. I have to go to the temple to help Caron, but you should stay here." A look through the yard door's peephole showed me a Crow inside the closed gate. Shan probably had the key, and there was only the one Crow. No crowd had gathered back here. Fear of the Crows' Hole must still sit strong in people's guts. The night sky flamed red. I swallowed hard. It looked like half the buildings between here and the Outer Circle were burning. Roth couldn't go out in that.

I looked over my shoulder at Roth. Was something wrong? He'd stopped giving orders. Instead he stood with his arms at his sides, looking at me like he'd never seen me before. Didn't he understand? "People are depending on me," I said.

Shan gave a soft laugh. "You've taught him well," she said to Roth. "It's annoying, isn't it?"

"What'll we do about the gate guard?" I asked.

Shan moved to the little table, which held a water bottle and a napkin crumpled over a dish. She handed me the stool and took the bottle and napkin.

"Miss Shandral?" called the Crow through the door. "Open the door. Please."

"I think I have the right key," Shan called back. "Oops. I dropped the whole ring. Just a moment. I'm sure I can find it again." She leaned down to whisper to me. "Wait until he takes off his helmet." She went out into the yard.

Heat from the fire flowed through the open door. I watched from behind it as the Crow spun to face her. He let go of his sword hilt when he saw who it was.

"If you're going to do this," Roth said, "at least be careful."

"Sure," I said. "Why don't you look after Jem for a while?" He couldn't help himself really.

Shan offered the water bottle to the gate guard. He took a long drink, and when he gave it back, she poured water onto the napkin and wiped his face. Then she said something, and he took off his helmet. She was wiping his forehead when I ran up and bashed the stool against the back of his head. For two heartbeats, nothing happened. Then his knees folded, and he collapsed face forward onto the cobblestones. I stared at his unconscious body. I had to do that.

I dropped the stool and bolted to where Shan was unlocking the gate. We ran along the narrow passages behind and beside Syndicate House. Smoke bit the back of my throat, and ashes floated down like black snow. Out front, the mob had shrunk to a handful of people, with fire light flickering red over their raised faces.

"Let us in," a man shouted, sounding hopeless.

Shan and I skirted around them, then tore through the streets, me already wondering desperately how to help Caron balance the stones. Water bubbled out of all the drains we passed and spread in widening puddles. We were halfway to the temple when lightning knifed the sky, thunder boomed, and icy rain beat down on us. The lane turned instantly into a river of mud. My feet shot out from under me, and I fell and floundered like a pig in a wallow. Shan pulled me up. My body reeled in confusion between the heat of the fire and the chill of the rain, but Mum's stone made a warm spot against my hip.

I glimpsed the temple spire as a rumble sounded over the pouring rain. I braced myself for a ground shaker, but as Shan and I spurted into the marketplace, I saw what was making the noise. A huge crowd swarmed between us and the ruined temple. Tricky gods. Now what?

We rocked to a halt on the edge of the mobbed marketplace. Panic flooded me. Driven by fear and the fire, anyone still in the city must have fled here. Rain poured down like it meant to beat us into mush.

"What's happening?" Shan asked a man in front of us.

"We heard there might be heart stones in the temple." The man was panting and shaking like a scared dog. "But the temple's been collapsing more each time the ground shakes. We can't get in."

I climbed on an abandoned market cart to see over the crowd. The temple's spire tipped toward us at a crazy angle, ready to wipe out the fools standing under it. "I don't see Caron," I said. "Do you think she's inside?"

"I hope so. We have to get to her."

How? There had to be a way. Think, Cade, think

My fingers tightened, and I realized I was gripping a wooden circle, part of a fallen balcony railing. Overhead, the balcony's slanting edge loomed only a few yards from the end of the temple spire. Yes! I stepped onto a circle and pulled myself up. Shan saw what I was doing and held the railing steady, glancing nervously over her shoulder at the crowd. It would be disastrous if anyone saw me climbing and came after me. If they got into the temple, they'd have all the stones gone between the start and end of the next lightning flash.

"Hurry," Shan murmured.

I scrambled onto the tipping balcony. The railing slid as Shan started to climb, and I strained to hold it while my feet skittered on the wet, crooked floor.

A man at the back of the crowd glanced toward us, and his mouth fell open. He took a step our way. "Can we get across?" he cried, loudly enough that several more people turned too.

Shan hopped up next to me. We both grabbed the railing and hauled on it, but the first man was on the bottom circle. Like a fool, he was watching me when Shan drove her heel into his forehead and knocked him backward. Shan and I dragged the railing out of reach.

"*Can* we get across?" Shan sat with her back against the wall, white-knuckled hands gripping the railing while people surged beneath us, looking for another way up.

"If we can brace the railing against the spire, we can."

She looked at the round, rain-slicked spire. "That looks dangerous."

Indeed it did. "I can do it, and it's me Caron needs."

She wiped her dripping hair out of her face and took a good look at the railing. Then she swung it out toward the spire. I moved to help her. The railing was light, but it was hard to control. The end bobbed over a sphere. We lowered it carefully, but it slid off, and we fell back trying to hang on.

"Move that way." Shan nudged me right. We slid on our backsides, fighting to stay on the slick balcony. When we lowered the end again, it wedged between two spheres.

Before I could decide it was stupid, I crawled out onto the railing. It sagged and creaked, but I gritted my teeth and kept going. Lightning flashed, and the hair lifted on the back of my neck. I was in a high place, in rain, in a lightning storm. I crawled on.

I was almost across, so I eyed the spire, looking for a landing place. I stretched one leg out and cautiously transferred some of my weight. The railing shot out from under me, then dropped into the crowd, shattering into pieces, with people shrieking and throwing up their arms to shield their heads.

I jumped the rest of the way and hugged the spire, but my foot skittered off the sphere, and I rolled sideways, frantically gripping with my knees. When I stopped moving, only empty air cushioned the space between me and the crowd. I swallowed my heart back down into my chest and pulled myself up to rest on the spire. Shan waved me to go on, then lowered herself off the far edge of the balcony and out of sight.

Lightning flashed again, showing faces gaping up at me.

It was a good thing Roth was still in the Crows' Hole. He'd be flinging railing pieces around and screaming about how stupid I was. I was already calling myself every name I could think of.

I took a deep breath and scooted backward from one sphere to the next. At last, I slithered off and collapsed onto a stone block. I was so thrilled at being safe that I couldn't move. Then, the block tipped, and I slid down, gathering speed. I grabbed and missed at every edge I whooshed past, trying to stop my rush to death. I shot under another block into darkness, then spun along a flat stone surface until I slammed into a rounded column. With all the air driven out of me, I lay there waiting for the floor to fall.

"Cade?" Caron bent over me. "Do you have the other stone?"

"I'm all right. Thank you for asking." I patted my pocket. Nothing. Had I dropped it on my sledding trip through the temple? I pulled the pocket inside out. Nothing!

I spat a curse word. How could I have come so far and lost the stone?

"Other pocket," Caron said.

And there it was, singing to me.

Caron snatched it from my fingers. "Help me."

The column I'd rammed into turned out to be the base of the altar. When the gods delivered a package, they did it right.

I climbed to my feet and looked at what Caron had done so far. Heart stones rested in eleven of the twelve hollows on the altar top, each of them thrumming with its own power and beating against the energy of the others. A shudder ran up my spine. The jangle of the stones hurt like a thousand pinpricks.

"Did you see Shan?" Caron asked. "Is she all right?"

"She's outside. I'd say she's all right. She told her father off. He was really mad."

Caron set Mum's stone in the last empty place on the altar. Fire flickered through the gaps in the ruins. The shouts of the crowd grew louder.

I longed to spread my arms over as many stones as I could reach, and yet my whole body flinched away from the altar. I wanted to hold a stone forever, and I wanted to run away until I couldn't feel the stones any more.

"Move the little one," I said.

Caron did, but it made no difference.

"Try the next hollow." I had to grind out the words.

Still the stones clashed. This was taking too long.

"It's not right." I elbowed Caron aside, snatched Mum's stone, and switched it with another. I had to pry my fingers off them, but I did it, mostly because the warring music of the other stones hurt enough to keep me from settling into the pull of whichever one I held.

The temple floor trembled. A huge stone block tipped over and crashed, its edge no more than a yard away. Rain and screaming voices flooded through the new opening.

"Go. This is for me to do." I swapped stones as fast as I could move them. It made no difference. My breathing got harder. My head spun every time I forced myself to let go of a stone.

"Can you do it?" Caron asked.

The ground shook so hard, my teeth clattered. A crack opened, and the floor tilted toward it. My feet skidded. I clung to the altar to keep from sliding into the earth.

"Get out!" I cried.

"If you can't do it, you get out too. We're in this together, and I'm not leaving you here to die alone. Can you do it?"

"I don't know!"

Caron grabbed my arm and pulled me uphill toward the black, starless sky. Leaving the stones behind made me hurt so bad that I couldn't stop her. All I could hear were my own scrambled thoughts. There were only twelve hollows. I was a Finder! I should have been able to do this, and yet I couldn't. People would die. Mum would die because I couldn't figure out how to make the stones work together.

The sound of shouts stabbed through my dazed pain. I stood next to Caron on top of a stone block. In front of us, rubble sloped down in a steep, unsteady hill. At the hill's bottom, people were shoving one another aside to try to climb. Some rich man's household servants pushed roughly through the crowd and swung sticks to drive everyone else away while the man they worked for scrambled up.

Lightning flashed, making the climbing man's white-blond hair glow. My stomach lurched. Malel, the mine owner who claimed to "own" Mum. And below him, held by a servant, was Mum, frail and lost in a churning crowd of strangers. Wilder must have caught her in our old neighborhood. I felt like I was once again dooming her because I couldn't manage a heart stone.

Malel struggled closer, still protected by his servants, the one holding Mum hauling her up the hill too. Her head was lowered, so she didn't see me, but Malel was close enough to shout to me. "You, boy, have you been in there? Get me a heart stone. I know they're in there." He pointed to Mum. "My Finder feels them."

"She's not 'yours,' you dung head," I cried.

Mum's head shot up, and for a crazed moment, I expected her to scold me for bad language. Our gazes met, and her face crumpled. "He said he had you and Roth. He said he'd kill you if I didn't help him." She slumped to her knees in the servant's grip, her hands over her face.

Malel looked from me to Mum. He whipped back to face me again and climbed another yard. "Get me a heart stone, and you can have her."

"Don't," Mum said.

The servant holding her yanked her erect, wrenching her arm so she cried out.

"Seize the boy," Malel shouted over his shoulder. "He's been in the temple. He knows where the stones are."

One of the servants turned uncertainly, still barring the crowd's way.

"Seize him, or I'll have you in prison," Malel said.

The servant had started up the crumbling hill when someone in a familiar fancy shirt shot out of the crowd, grabbed Malel's foot, and sent him sprawling. I could barely believe it. Keled hated my guts and was mad at Shan because she lied, but he'd evidently decided we were worth helping.

The ground shook again. Caron started picking her way down the slope, tugging at me so I nearly dropped the stone I hadn't realized I still held. Mum's stone, I saw, the one I'd given her so she wound up in Malel's mine. If I took it down there and hung onto Mum, maybe it would save us the way it saved Roth when he was sick. I looked again at Mum's anguished face, adrift in a sea of anguished faces. A wall of fire rose over the roof tops.

I looked back into the temple in time for a lightning flash to show me the murals, looking terrifyingly like what was in front of me.

I closed my fist around the stone, shook Caron's hand off, and dove back into the ruins. I had to be able to keep disaster from happening. The gods wouldn't have made me and Mum and Jem into Finders, just so some mine owner could grow rich off us.

I skidded down the slanting floor so fast I was zooming past the altar before I saw it. I grabbed at it and jerked to a halt with a yank that nearly tore my arm out. Mum's stone rolled to my fingertips, then teetered on my nails. No! I tipped my hand, coaxing it. The stone danced on my fingertips like it was teasing me. Then it settled in my palm. Before I did anything else, I dropped it safely onto the altar top. I had trouble letting go, but then the stone seemed to jump out of my hand. To hold myself steady, I wrapped one arm around the altar's edge and dug my toes into the crack between the floor and the column holding the altar. The top was still level. Its column must run deep, not resting on the floor but running through it. The stones on the altar trembled with their own clashing energy, not the shaking of the earth.

This close to them, even my teeth prickled with pain. Using only a fingernail, I nudged Mum's stone into the one empty hollow. The clang of the stones grew worse. My vision blurred, and it took me a moment to realize that was because I was crying.

I closed my eyes, but I couldn't shut out the hurt. Of course not. Being able to sense heart stones beyond sight was what made a Finder. Why had the gods done that? What did they want from me? I imagined them waiting, holding their breaths to see if I could figure a way to save everyone outside this temple, the ones I loved, the ones I hated, and the ones I didn't even know.

With my eyes still shut, I groped for a stone. My hand brushed one and knocked it out of its hollow. My pain spurted. My hand was hovering over the stone, ready to put it back, when my pain ebbed a little. I hurt less with the stone where it was. Was it possible that was where it belonged?

I felt around for more stones. The next one I touched made me cringe. I slid it around on the altar top until the feel of it softened.

Thunder boomed, and through my closed eyelids, I saw the lightning. The temple shook again. The noise of the crowd swelled.

I raced my hand over the altar, finding and moving stones, feeling my way with my hand and my heart. I left two stones in hollows, but set the rest on the altar top. Maybe the altar's makers had got it wrong. Or maybe they'd got it right, and the altar had shifted over the centuries. Whatever. I had to ignore the pre-made places and find new ones. For a world that was changing, that seemed right anyway. The stones began to hum in harmony. I was almost there.

"Midnight!" someone outside shouted. "It's midnight."

I coaxed the last stone closer to the center and opened my eyes. The stones' hum burst into a song that any Finder within a league would hear. It was like water and birdsong and the sweetest of fiddles all blending together in a glorious burst of music. Hearing it made my heart and the rest of me too leap with joy whose source I didn't understand. The floor steadied. I held my breath.

A loud crack shattered the air. I jumped, and my heart burst into a gallop. A spear of light shot from the center of the altar, stretching into the sky and, I could feel, into the earth too. It was power, and it was pinning us all in place as the world wrenched itself out of its old direction and into some new one.

Good or bad?

I'd soon find out.

20. TRIAL

All travelers are tested.—Geat, the gatekeeper god

Power flowed from the pillar of light and flooded every remaining inch of the temple. The floor heaved in waves, pushing me toward the place where I'd last seen Caron. A chunk of the roof creaked.

I can take a hint as well as the next person. I skated to where the temple was sending me, then hurled myself outside to roll down the hill of rubble, banging shoulder, elbow, and knee against stone before finally coming to rest. Rain washed over me. I lay on my side staring at the column of light. All around me, the crowd's wails hushed to a frightened, awestruck silence.

The light flared bright enough to make me squint. So quickly it was hard to believe it happened, the remains of the temple roof spun down and its floor spun up. With an ear-battering crash, the two snapped together like a closing clam shell, then collapsed flat. The column of light was sucked in, taking the rain with it. The roar of the fire snapped out, and its light vanished. Stars burst into view. The rubble I lay on slid and evened out to a field of broken stone in the middle of the market.

I was so stunned, I couldn't speak. Not Shan, though. She climbed onto the biggest chunk of rubble, with Caron hovering nearby. As I struggled to climb to my feet, Shan spoke loudly enough for the whole crowd to hear.

"People of Cor City, the gods have preserved us. As our governor's daughter, and in your names, I thank them and those who carried out the gods' plans."

I was sure it was a good speech, but I had more important things to think about. I clambered across the rubble toward Mum, and no one stopped her from stumbling to meet me. Malel was staring open-mouthed at the empty place where the temple had been, and the servant who'd held her had let go and, like half the people there, dropped to his knees. Mum was crying and laughing as she flung her arms around me. "Cade! I thought I'd never see you again."

She was so thin! She felt fragile as a bird inside my hug. But her voice was the same. She was the same. And she was safe. I'd sent her into torment, but now I'd saved her and everyone else here.

Shan shouted my name. "We owe much to people like Cade. The gods made the plans, but they needed help to carry them out. They needed Finders like these two." She pointed to me and Mum. "So in Governor Barth's name, I declare that all Finders shall be free to accept or refuse what work they like because their gift saved us." She beckoned to me and Mum, and when I came up next to her, she laid her hand on top of my head. I clutched hold of Mum, who was scarily unsteady on her feet.

A wordless cheer started low and swelled as the crowd slowly let go of their terror.

"Wait." Still trailed by Keled, Malel marched toward us. "This woman belongs to me. You have no right to say otherwise."

So balancing the heart stones hadn't fixed everything. Mean people were still mean. I put myself between Malel and Mum. "Belongs? I'll cram your 'belong' up your—" I glanced at Mum. "—down your throat if you set one toe closer."

Though Malel was a good foot taller than me, his face went gray. He looked around for his servants, but they were watching Shan, who'd lifted her hand to show she had more to say. "The Finders couldn't have done this alone. We also owe thanks to generous miners who gave up their own heart stones for the good of everyone, miners like Malel here." She gave Malel an evil smile.

He darted his eyes side to side, like a scared rabbit. Keled hooked his arm around Malel's shoulders and led him toward the cheering mob.

"Malel! Malel!" the crowd chanted.

The cheers made me want to puke. At least Malel was out of our way for now, but it turned out he wasn't our worst problem. A Crow struggled free of the crowd and picked his way across the rubble toward Shan. When I recognized Wilder, I tightened my grip on Mum. Shan must have seen trouble on its way too, because she braced herself on Caron's shoulder, climbed down from her perch, and came next to me.

"Miss Shandral," Wilder said, "I've been searching for you. Your father is very worried. He wants you home." He grabbed my arm. "And you're under arrest." He jerked his chin at Caron. "You get away. You're no longer welcome in Syndicate House."

"I see you're still kissing Governor Barth's backside, Wilder," Caron said.

Shan grinned. "I'm on my way home now, Wilder. And when I tell my father how my friends and I saved the city, he'll grant what I've promised in his name, and let Cade go."

"If you say so, Miss," Wilder said, with a patronizing smile. He needed kicking, and I wished with everything in me that I could be the one to do it.

I gripped Mum's hand. "She stays with me." I sure wasn't going to leave her with Malel.

Wilder frowned at Mum. "When she didn't have the governor's stone, I returned her to Malel. I have no orders to bring her."

Shan stuck out her jaw. "Wilder, Cade's mother comes with us, or I tell this whole crowd that you're abusing the Finders who saved us."

"Take a look around, Wilder," Caron said. "Just now, these people like Finders much more than they like you. Why, they might just demand Cade's and his mother's freedom right now. How would you explain that to the governor?"

Wait. Shan had just said we were free. It occurred to me that she didn't have the power to make that stick. Gods help me. Had I just saved the city and condemned my family anyway?

Wilder glanced at the faces around us. Folks kept a yard back from us, but they were frowning at Wilder and muttering to one another.

Shan leaned to speak in Caron's ear. Wilder moved closer, trying to hear, but the scowl on his face said he had no luck. Caron nodded, then strolled to a knot of women and began speaking to them.

Shan turned to Wilder. "It's your choice, Wilder." She smiled sweetly, which would have worried me if I were him. "You and I can escort Cade and his mother to Syndicate House, or I can get back on that rock and talk again."

Wilder took one more quick look around. "Fine. Bring her." He tightened his grip on me and offered his free arm to Shan, who took Mum's instead. Wilder hustled us away while the crowd was busy. "I can't believe the temple really had power." He gave a shaky laugh. "I was scared to go in there when I was a kid. My friends dared me and then hid and jumped out at me."

"You saw what just happened, and you're still hauling us off to the governor?" I said desperately. "That was gods' work."

"The gods are stingy with coin," Wilder said. "The governor pays me. Keep moving." The voices of the crowd faded behind us as Wilder took us through a spring night that was suddenly sweet, despite the way we had to detour around cracked earth and the charred wrecks of houses and shops. The air was soft and smelled like growing things.

I held on to Mum every step of the way, my brain scurrying uselessly after a way to save her and Roth.

Syndicate House was undamaged, so the governor's giant heart stone had done its work, and Roth and Jem at least hadn't burned or fallen into the earth. The front gates were battered and bent, but still there. When the Crow on guard saw Shan, he hurried to open the small gate set into one side.

"Good night, Miss," Wilder said. "You go on in, and I'll take these two around back."

Shan kept hold of Mum. "Cade and his mother come this way too."

Wilder heaved a sigh like a man who was heavily put upon, then shoved me through the gate after Shan. Only the one Crow was in the yard. The others must be collapsed at home, nursing their hurts and rejoicing that their families were still alive.

Shan led us down the wide front hall to a small chamber outside the heartroom. Wilder rolled his eyes when he saw where she meant to put us.

"They're prisoners, Miss," he moaned.

Ignoring him, Shan eased Mum into a cushioned chair before speaking to me. "Don't worry," she said. "I'm going to talk to my father. He has to be grateful for what we did. He has to."

She sounded way too uncertain to ease the knot in my stomach.

Shan left. Glaring at me and Mum, Wilder moved to block the door. A moment later, someone knocked and Wilder let in a servant girl who gave towels to Mum and me so we could blot off some of the rain. When she left, she ignored the scowling Wilder who was dripping onto the carpet.

Mum put her hand out to me. "Tell me what's happened," she said. "Where's Roth?"

I sat on the floor next to her and tried to explain without upsetting her too much. Given that Roth was in the Crows' Hole and I'd been thieving, that was tricky. As I went along, she looked less and less happy.

Wilder listened too. When I finished telling about the altar in the temple, he snorted and said, "I don't care what you did. You're still a Finder and don't belong with decent folks."

"Keep quiet," Mum said sharply. "That way no one will know you're a dung head."

I choked back a laugh.

Wilder was still gaping at her when the door opened and Captain Menard beckoned to Wilder. Wilder went out into the hallway where Menard gave him some order I didn't hear. Wilder left, and Menard came in. He nodded to Mum, then spoke to me.

"The word is you went into the old temple and used heart stones to stop the chaos and fever."

"Shan figured out we could use the stones in the temple." I bit back the urge to say Shan was the one who'd gathered the stones too, because accusing Governor Barth's daughter of stealing heart stones seemed like a bad idea.

"Then the city should thank you," he said. "My wife was safe here, but I have friends and family who would have died if you hadn't managed it."

"He's earned a reward," Mum said. "The question is whether the governor will give him one."

Menard's mouth tightened. "We're about to find out. Governor Barth is ready to hold a trial. This way, please." He held the door open for us and then directed us into the heartroom I'd been in only a couple of hours ago. Governor Barth's chair was empty, but Menard pointed for us to stand in front of it. The room felt huge, like it was designed to make me and Mum feel small.

Footsteps sounded outside a different entrance. My breath caught in my throat, but it wasn't Governor Barth who came in. It was Roth and Jem, herded through by Wilder.

Despite Wilder's prodding, Roth stopped dead, then rushed toward us. "Mum!"

She put a trembling hand on his face.

"Don't cry," he said. "Please don't cry."

Jem came to stand next to me. He looked exhausted, his brown curls dangling limply in his face. "Are Keled and Caron all right?"

"The last time I saw Keled, he was baiting a mine owner," I said.

Jem smiled faintly. "Then he was enjoying himself."

Everyone I was worried about was there. Might we be able to overpower Menard and Wilder and escape before the governor came? I looked sideways at them. Wilder watched us with narrowed eyes, hand on the hilt of his sword. And Menard might think I'd done a good thing, but he still looked like an experienced Crow, alert and ready to move if he had to. We'd never get out without someone being hurt, probably Mum or Jem.

More footsteps echoed, and Governor Barth swept into the room with Shan at his heels. He looked mad enough to eat nails. Dark half moons stained the skin under his eyes, but he was shaven and cleanly dressed in black wool trousers and wide-collared grey silk shirt. My heart thudded. This foul-tempered man held our fate in his hands. He seated himself in his big chair. Shan stood next to him, biting her lip. I swallowed hard. She looked ready to cry like Mum. That couldn't be good.

The governor's gaze swept along the row of us and landed on me. I felt like someone had crammed a snowball down my shirt.

"Given what happened in this house two hours ago, there's no doubt that you, at least, are a Finder, and one willing to commit violence," he said in that non-mouth moving way of his. "But they'll manage you at the mine. And I understand that these two have owners to whom I can simply return them." He waved at Mum and Jem, the jewels on his fingers flashing in the lantern light.

"Nobody owns them." My voice cracked with despair.

The governor acted like he hadn't heard me. Instead, he cocked his head, as if listening to something else. I realized a noise like wind had been growing. It almost sounded like another ground shaker. But how could that be? The weather should be back to normal.

Governor Barth brought his attention back to Roth. "You, on the other hand, are a simple thief, caught with a stolen heart stone. Hanging you will save us the cost of your keep."

Roth pulled Mum tighter against him, face bleak as a winter sky. She dug her fingers into his shirt like she'd never let go.

"You can't do any of that," Shan said. "If you don't keep your promises, people will say you went back on your word."

"Your promises, not mine," the governor said.

"Don't you even care that I saved the city?" Shan's voice trembled. "Don't you care that I saved you?"

"I care that you were foolish," Governor Barth said sharply.

Shan hugged herself and turned away.

The rumble outside rose louder. Then I noticed what I should have noticed before, what I would have noticed if I hadn't been so worried. I noticed the thing that wasn't there.

"Menard, Wilder," the governor said, "take them—"

"Mum, do you feel a heart stone?" I interrupted.

She raised her head from Roth's shoulder. "No."

"Jem?" I asked.

He shook his head. "I felt one all the while I was in the Crows' Hole, but then, a little while ago, it was gone."

Governor Barth's eyes widened. He jumped to his feet and crossed to the altar, fumbling a small key from his belt. He unlocked and opened the jeweled box. His huge heart stone gleamed, but I felt nothing, and from the puzzled looks on their faces, neither did Mum or Jem.

"Is it one of your fakes, Shan?" I asked.

She shook her head. "Keled never made a match for it. He said making glass perfectly round like that was very difficult."

"It's just a stone," I said. "Just rock." I didn't understand. The only other times I'd seen heart stones so lifeless, they'd been stuck in shrines. My breath caught. Shrines built by the same people who'd built the temple. "Tricky gods. Did I do that?"

Governor Barth took two menacing steps toward me. "Did you do what?"

"I'm not sure," I said, "but when Finders put heart stones into a shrine, they give back the Gift of Finding. I'm just wondering if maybe when I arranged the stones in the temple, I gave back the Gift for all of us."

Governor Barth went pale. "That can't be."

"In the shrines, the stones lose power too," I said.

"No!" Governor Barth cried. "Half our syndicate's wealth comes from selling those stones." He staggered back to his chair. "It can't be true. Gods help me. If it is, we'll lose control of the governorship."

The noise outside had changed from a steady roar to what sounded like pounding and chanting. "Go see what that is, Wilder," Captain Menard said. Wilder left the room.

Governor Barth gripped the arms of his chair. "No one outside this room needs to know. I can stop every tongue here."

"Not mine," Shan said.

"It might not be so bad," I said. "Heart stones won't heal any more, which is a loss, but people might want them like they want the miners' diamonds, because they're pretty and rare. Maybe they'll even want them more because of what happened in the temple tonight. The only thing is, you won't be able to use Finders to mine them because we're not Finders any more."

Wilder ran through the doorway, breathing hard. "Captain, there's a big crowd battering in the gate. They want to see Cade so they can be sure he's all right. Caron is there egging them on. And there's a man demanding to see Jem too."

Shan's face relaxed into a smug smile. She'd done this, I realized. This was what she'd told Keled and Caron to do when we were leaving the temple.

Governor Barth swore. "Drive them away."

"I have so few men here, I'm not sure I can, sir," Captain Menard said.

"The gates were weakened last night." Wilder's voice shook. "They're bending. That crowd will be in here if we don't do something."

Shan's smile faded into a look of alarm. She put a hand on her father's shoulder.

I had a quick vision of people rioting into this room and taking their anger out on Governor Barth and felt a spurt of vengeful satisfaction, followed by a flush of shame. What kind of person was I? Tonight seemed to be the night for deciding.

Besides when I saw Shan's distressed face, I couldn't do it. Her father was mean to her, but she loved him anyway. That didn't seem right to me, but sometimes folks were too mixed up for me to untangle all the threads.

"We can go out and talk to people," I offered. "You can even talk to them yourself. Tell them you'll keep Shan's promises. They'll like that."

The governor hesitated.

The noise from outside grew louder. Wilder swallowed noisily and ran from the room. I doubted he meant to join the sole Crow in the yard.

"Those gates won't hold, sir," Captain Menard said.

"Oh, what does it matter? The stones have gone dead." Governor Barth's voice was anguished. "Take them outside, Captain."

The captain hurried to usher Mum, Roth, Jem, and me out of the room and out of Syndicate House. I got the impression he thought we shouldn't linger, just in case Governor Barth got hold of himself again and noticed he was letting a chance for meanness get away. I looked back to see Shan at her father's side, her arm around him, his face buried in her shoulder.

21. NEW YEAR

The world gleams new everywhere I look.—Cild, the child god
    A month later, I knocked on Granny's door and handed her the food. When she carried it in and set it on her small table, I followed so I could hug Mum, who was staying with Granny for now. Caron was there too, which probably meant Shan was at our house. Shan still lived with her father, though they'd moved out of Syndicate House, but she spent most of her days with Caron.

Mum put aside the sewing she was doing for Shan. "How was work?"

"Good. Did Roth get a job today?" A week after New Year, Elgar had taken me back, but Roth's old foreman had bad-mouthed him, and he was having trouble finding anyone who'd hire him. Even with what Shan paid Mum, we were short on coin.

"I saw Roth go past," Mum said, "but I haven't spoken to him yet. He's probably talking to Shan."

If talking was going on at our house, Shan was the one doing it.

Granny cackled. "Maybe we should keep Cade here."

Mum laughed, but said, "Go on now, Cade."

I kissed her forehead and left. As I passed our open window, I was surprised to hear a man's voice. I went in to find Shan sitting demurely, hands folded on the table, watching Roth and a gray-haired man, who was the one speaking. From the back, I didn't recognize him, but Roth's face was tense with excitement.

At the sound of my coming in, the man turned, and I recognized the high-cheeked face with its day's-end shadow of a dark beard: Master Duval, the lawyer Roth had been apprenticed to, the one who'd betrayed us.

Roth spoke quickly, like he was afraid of what I might say. "Cade, you remember Master Duval? He's told me how mistaken we were when we thought he'd sent for the Watch."

I puffed out some air.

"I believe him," Roth said sharply.

I hesitated, trying to remember exactly what had happened in Duval's office. Maybe the voice we'd heard really had been a client's. I decided if Roth believed Duval, then I did too.

"Good evening, sir," I said, extra polite.

Duval smiled at me. "I've been hearing about you, young man. You did a brave thing."

My face got hot, and I smiled at my feet. "Thank you."

Duval turned back to Roth. "If we're agreed then, you can start work tomorrow."

I looked up to see Roth grinning so widely, his ears probably moved farther apart. This was good. I shared a gleeful look with Shan.

Duval stood up, and Roth did too, coming around the table to escort Duval to the door. "You'll have a long walk from here," Duval said. "Why not stay with me?"

"No," I blurted. Roth's gaze shifted from Duval to me. "I mean," I said hastily, "if that's better for you, Roth, of course you should do it." I could see him on his days off, I told myself. I should stop being so selfish, even if I had just barely gotten used to having my family whole again.

Shan drifted up next to Roth watching him with a half smile, like she had a secret thought.

"Thank you, Master Duval," Roth said, "but I can manage the walk. Anyway, if I'm working again, then I mean to talk to my mother and brother about moving back to Sceld's Gate. There's a stablemaster who'd probably be happy to have Cade working for him again."

For a moment, I froze, making sure he said what I thought he said. "Yes!" I cried. "Shan, you'll still visit us won't you? And maybe we should take Granny with us. No one seems to be looking after her."

Roth laughed. "We'll see what Granny and Mum say."

Duval was smiling too. "Until tomorrow then, Roth." He opened the door.

"Master Duval?" Roth put his hand on my shoulder. Duval turned, one eyebrow raised. "I love the law for the order it makes," Roth said, "but it should make justice too. The law should be better."

Duval glanced at me, his face sobering. "Yes, it should. We'll have to see what we can do." He went out, closing the door behind him.

Shan tapped a finger on her pursed lips. "You're a good man, Roth, Mareth's son."

Roth went red all the way to his forehead.

I looked from him to Shan and back. "You two should go tell Mum about this," I said. "You know. Go together." Roth would never get anywhere on his own, and really, what are brothers for?

Roth narrowed his eyes, but Shan laughed. "You're right," she said. "Come on, Roth." She grabbed his hand and dragged him out of the house.

Whistling, I put the rest of my food on our table. I didn't need to be rich as a miner or jeweler to be happy. Even miners and jewelers didn't need that. Some of them like Keled weren't rich anyway, but he seemed content enough living with Jem and his cat and going back to glasswork. Besides, no one was always happy. No one had things their way all the time. You fought for what you cared about, and even when you won, you still had to get up and fight again the next day. The syndicates were meeting tomorrow to choose a new governor. We'd have to see what that one was like.

For now, though, I had what I wanted. Roth and Mum were safe. I had found what mattered to me, and other people were better off because of me too. Mum says sometimes happiness creeps up on you while you're thinking about something else.

The gods are tricky.

ABOUT THE AUTHOR

Dorothy A. Winsor is originally from Detroit but moved to Iowa in 1995. She still blinks when she sees a cornfield outside her living room window. For about a dozen years, she taught technical writing at Iowa State University and served as the editor of the Journal of Business and Technical Communication. Before that, she taught for ten years at GMI Engineering & Management Institute (now Kettering). She's won six national awards for outstanding research on the communication practices of engineers. She lives with her husband, who engineers tractors, and has one son, the person who first introduced her to the pleasure of reading fantasy. *Finders Keepers* is her first novel. It was a finalist in the e-book fiction category of the Eric Hoffer Awards. Her young adult fantasy, *Deep as a Tomb* (Loose Leaves Publishing), will be available in November, 2016.

If you enjoyed *Finders Keepers*, consider leaving a review online.

Made in the USA
Monee, IL
06 November 2019